THE PERFECT NEW YEAR'S EVE

"We have something for you two," Stevie said. "It's sort of a Christmas present. Well, more of a New Year's Eve present, really. Let's just call it a holiday present."

"For us?" Max took the envelope, looking mystified. He slit it open with his thumb and pulled out the card.

"What is it, Max?" Deborah asked curiously.

"Look at this," he told her. "The girls want to baby-sit for us on New Year's Eve while we go out."

"We made reservations for you and everything," Lisa said in a rush. "And we'll come to your house and watch Maxi the whole time you're gone."

Carole bit her lip. She couldn't stand the suspense. After all The Saddle Club had done, were Max and Deborah going to say no?

Stevie obviously thought so. "Listen," she said, "I don't care what arguments you have against this. We think—"

Max and Deborah didn't let her finish. They both spoke up at once. "We'll take it!" they said quickly.

Other books you will enjoy

THE SADDLE CLUB

HOLIDAY HORSE

BONNIE BRYANT

A SKYLARK BOOK
NEW YORK • TORONTO • LONDON • SYDNEY • AUCKLAND

RL 5, 009–012

HOLIDAY HORSE

A Bantam Skylark Book / December 1997

ISBN 0-553-48427-3

Published simultaneously in the United States and Canada.

PRINTED IN THE UNITED STATES OF AMERICA

OPM   0 9 8 7 6 5 4 3 2

*I would like to express my special thanks
to Catherine Hapka for her help
in the writing of this book.*

"WHAT ABOUT AN egg-and-spoon race?" Carole Hanson suggested.

Lisa Atwood wrinkled her nose. "Too boring. We've done it a thousand times already."

Carole gave a gentle tug on the lead line she was holding. Her horse, Starlight, had stopped to examine a clod of dirt lying on the floor of the indoor ring of Pine Hollow Stables. He wasn't supposed to be stopping. He was supposed to be walking. Carole was cooling him down after a strenuous hour of exercise.

"True," Carole said once Starlight was moving again. "But it's always fun."

Lisa grinned. "Remember the last gymkhana, when Stevie slipped a raw egg in with the hard-boiled ones?"

"How could I forget?" Carole said with a laugh. "Veronica diAngelo complained about the stains on her expensive new boots for a month. Right, Stevie?"

There was no answer.

"Stevie?" Lisa prompted. She glanced over the back of her horse, a pretty Thoroughbred mare named Prancer, at the third human member of their group. "Earth to Stevie!"

Stevie Lake was walking her horse along with her friends, but she wasn't paying attention to the conversation. Lisa had to call her name several more times before Stevie finally looked up blankly. "What?" she asked, pushing a stray lock of dark blond hair out of her eyes. "Were you talking to me?"

Carole and Lisa exchanged a look and a sigh.

"Don't tell me you're still thinking about Phil," Carole said.

Lisa switched Prancer's lead line to her other hand. "You've been brooding about it all week," she added.

Stevie's boyfriend, Phil Marsten, was leaving on a family vacation the next morning. Normally that wouldn't have bothered Stevie very much, since Phil lived in another town and she only saw him once or twice a month. But New Year's Eve was a few days away, and Stevie had been hoping that she and Phil would be able to spend the holiday together.

2

"Can you blame me for being upset about it?" she asked her friends. "The Marstens invited me to come to Disney World with them, you know. I could be ringing in the new year in the Magic Kingdom. Instead, I'm stuck here in the frozen kingdom."

Willow Creek, Virginia, where Stevie, Carole, and Lisa lived, was experiencing a severe cold snap. The three girls hadn't been able to ride outdoors that day because of the frigid weather. Instead, they had spent an hour riding in Pine Hollow's indoor ring. Their regular riding lessons were on hiatus during the holidays, but the girls still made sure to ride regularly—for at least three good reasons.

The first reason was to keep their horses in shape. Carole and Stevie owned their horses, and Lisa was almost as attached to Prancer, a stable horse, as if the mare belonged to her. It was important for the horses to get out of their stalls and stretch their legs. The exercise kept them fit, and it kept them happy.

The second reason was Pine Hollow's upcoming gymkhana. A gymkhana was a kind of informal horse show in which teams of young riders competed in riding games and races. Max Regnery, Pine Hollow's owner and the girls' riding instructor, had announced the event at their last lesson before Christmas. It was now less than three weeks away. Max had also asked all the young riders to come up with ideas for gymkhana events. The girls knew that in addition to being fun, the games would test the riding skills they had been learning and practicing in their lessons, and they wanted to be ready.

The third reason for riding was the best and simplest one of all. Stevie, Carole, and Lisa loved to ride. In fact, they loved horses and riding so much that they had formed The Saddle Club. The group had only two rules: Members had to be horse-crazy, and they had to be willing to help each other out whenever help was needed. With three horse-crazy best friends as club members, both rules were easy to keep. The girls had even added a few out-of-town members to The Saddle Club, including Phil Marsten.

"It was nice of Phil's parents to invite you," Lisa said, brushing a fly off Prancer's withers. "But I'm not surprised your parents said you couldn't go."

Carole rolled her eyes. "Me neither," she said. "Your folks weren't exactly amused by that Christmas gift you gave Chad."

"Oh, that," Stevie said, waving one hand dismissively. Chad was one of her three brothers. "It was only what he deserved."

"Maybe so," Lisa said dryly. "But how many parents want their son unwrapping a big package of horse manure in the middle of the living room floor on Christmas morning?"

"It was very nicely wrapped," Stevie said with a grin. "And by the way, it was Veronica's own fault she got egg on her boots. I didn't make her drop it, did I?"

Her friends looked blank for a moment. Then they laughed. Although they had been best friends for quite a while, sometimes the way Stevie's mind worked still amazed them.

Carole and Lisa were also often astounded at the various ways Stevie managed to get into trouble. If she wasn't fighting with her brothers, she was teasing Veronica diAngelo, the snobbiest girl at Pine Hollow, or playing pranks at school.

Lisa, especially, was very studious and responsible. She couldn't imagine how Stevie got away with half the things she did. "It's too bad you pulled that prank on Chad so recently," she said. "Otherwise you might be flying off to sunny Florida tomorrow."

Stevie shrugged. "I didn't have a choice," she said. "I had to pay Chad back for taping my phone conversation with Phil and playing it over the school PA system."

Lisa still looked unconvinced, but Carole smiled and said, "True. Besides, didn't you say yesterday that the main reason you can't go to Florida is because your grandmother is coming to visit?"

"Well, maybe," Stevie admitted. "She's coming in two weeks. And for some reason my parents seem to think it will take me that long to clean up my room."

Her friends laughed. They had seen Stevie's room many times. They had even helped to clean it up on more than one occasion. And they couldn't help agreeing with Mr. and Mrs. Lake—it was always a big job.

5

"Think of it this way, Stevie," Carole said in a comforting tone. She reached over to pat Stevie's horse, a spirited bay mare named Belle. "You may miss going to Disney World with Phil, but at least this way you'll get to spend part of New Year's Eve with Belle."

Carole looked surprised when Stevie and Lisa both started to laugh. Then she laughed, too. Of the three horse-crazy girls, Carole was famous for being the horse-craziest. Her first priority was always horses, which some people found strange. But not Stevie and Lisa. It was one of the things they loved most about their friend.

"Carole's right," Lisa said. "Even if you don't get to celebrate the New Year with Phil, at least you have Belle—and us. Maybe it's not Disney World, but I'm sure we'll still manage to have fun."

Stevie nodded. "We always do," she said, smiling at her two best friends. "I'd rather talk to you guys than to Mickey Mouse, anyway." The three girls had already decided to have a Saddle Club sleepover on New Year's Eve. "And there's lots to do. We can play games—"

"Talk about the gymkhana—" Carole added.

"Come up with New Year's resolutions—" Lisa continued.

"—and make prank phone calls to my brothers," Stevie finished with satisfaction. "A perfect way to end any year."

"Oops," Carole said, suddenly looking worried.

"What's the matter?" Stevie asked, peering around Belle at her friend.

"I forgot to tell you," Carole said. "I was so busy think-ing about the gymkhana that it slipped my mind. I have some bad news." She shook her head. "Well, not really *bad* news—I mean, it's kind of bad for us—well, inconve-nient more than bad, really—it's actually kind of good news for my dad. But—"

"Carole!" Lisa said sharply. "Just tell us already. What is it?" On any topic but horses, Carole could be a little absentminded. Sometimes she'd start a sentence and for-get to end it.

Carole looked sheepish. "Sorry. What I'm trying to say is, we can't have the sleepover at my house after all. My dad has a date. He's got reservations at this really fancy restaurant in the city."

Stevie shrugged. "So? We're old enough. We don't need a baby-sitter."

"I know," Carole said. "And my dad knows that, too. It's not that he wouldn't trust us to stay alone. But I'm afraid that if he knew we were going to be at my house, he'd feel like he had to cancel his plans and hang out with us. And I know that we'd all have fun, but . . ."

Lisa nodded sympathetically. She and Stevie both knew that Carole's father, Colonel Hanson, had casually dated a few different women since Carole's mother had died a couple of years earlier. But he hadn't been on any

New Year's Eve dates at fancy city restaurants. That sounded really romantic to Lisa. "He's skittish, huh?" she asked.

"A little," Carole said. "I don't want to give him an excuse to back out. I think he should go out and have a good time—you know, with other grown-ups."

"Got it," Lisa said briskly. "So your place is out. No problem—we'll go to Stevie's."

Stevie was already shaking her head. "More bad news," she said grimly. "And this time there's no two ways about it. It's *really* bad. My parents told me this morning." She paused dramatically. "They gave Chad permission to have a New Year's Eve party for all his creepy friends."

"Ugh," Carole said. "So much for that idea. We don't want to be anywhere near that party."

Lisa laughed. "Right. Not unless we want to spend the whole night watching Stevie and Chad sneaking live toads into each other's beds."

"Oh, please," Stevie said with a sniff. "Toads, indeed. I think I can be a little more creative than that."

"That's what I'm afraid of," Lisa said. "Anyway, I wish we could stay at my house. But my parents are going to a party on New Year's Eve. And you know how my mother is."

The other two girls just nodded. Mrs. Atwood was a worrier, and she tended to be overprotective of Lisa.

"Even though she lets me baby-sit for other people all

the time, she'd probably insist on calling a nanny service to come and stay with us," Lisa said with a sigh. She knew that didn't sound very logical, but her mother wasn't always the most logical person in the world.

"Too bad it's so cold," Stevie said. "Otherwise we could ask Max to let us sleep in the loft." The hayloft at Pine Hollow was one of the girls' favorite spots for a sleepover—but only in warm weather. The stable itself was well heated, but the loft was drafty and could be chilly when a winter wind was blowing.

"Well, we'll have to come up with something," Carole said. "I guess if we have to, we can still have the sleepover at my house."

Stevie could tell that Carole wasn't thrilled about that option. She decided it was time to change the subject. "Hey, I want to try something," she said. "I had an idea for a gymkhana event, but I'm not sure it will work."

"What is it?" Carole asked, immediately looking interested.

"It's sort of a leading race," Stevie said. "The teams would have to see how many horses they could lead in a row from one lead horse and rider."

"You mean like packhorses on a trail?" Carole asked.

Stevie nodded. "What do you think? Can we try doing it right now?"

Carole looked at the three horses doubtfully. "To be honest, I'm not sure it will work. Those packhorses get special training to learn to follow the lead horse. These guys might not even understand what we're trying to get them to do."

"Especially Prancer," Lisa said, sounding a little anxious. Prancer had originally been trained as a racehorse. She had started her new career as a school horse fairly recently, and although she had taken to it quickly, she wasn't as steady and experienced as many of the other horses at Pine Hollow. And as a typically hot-blooded Thoroughbred, she sometimes got nervous and skittish when asked to do something new.

"Well, maybe experimenting with Prancer isn't such a good idea," Stevie agreed. "But we could try it with Belle and Starlight, right?"

Carole brought Starlight to a halt. She felt the skin on the gelding's chest, right between his front legs. That was the easiest way she knew to tell whether his body temperature had returned to normal. "Okay," she said. "He's cool. I guess we can try it."

Lisa led Prancer a short distance away to watch. "Do you want me to get a longer lead line from the tack room?" she asked.

Carole shook her head. "I think I remember how to do a tail hitch," she said. "This line should be long enough if we do it that way. And Starlight almost never kicks, so it shouldn't be dangerous for Belle. Should I try it?" All three girls had learned about tail hitches in their Pony Club meetings. Max had explained that a tail hitch was a common method of hitching packhorses together on the trail. The girls had also seen the method used at the Bar None Ranch out West.

"Go for it," Stevie said. She handed Belle's lead line to Carole.

Carole took the line and, while Stevie took Starlight's line, walked to her horse's hindquarters, running one hand along his side to let him know where she was. Then she picked up his tail.

Starlight swung his head around and peered at her over his shoulder. He seemed curious but trusting. After handling the horse's tail for another few moments, Carole carefully gathered the strands together and looped Belle's lead line around them. Before long she had the line firmly knotted around Starlight's tail, which was folded back on itself to make a neat, compact package.

Belle had her ears pricked forward. When Carole stepped back a little, the mare stretched her head toward Starlight's tail and snorted. Starlight turned around again and gazed at Belle with what Carole would have sworn was a look of mild surprise.

"What do you think, boy?" she asked, giving her horse a pat on the hindquarters. "Do you like being in the lead?"

"Try walking him around," Stevie suggested. "See if Belle will follow him."

Carole went to Starlight's head and led him forward a few steps. Belle snorted again as her lead line tightened.

To decrease the chance of injury, Carole had been careful to leave the rope short enough so that the mare couldn't possibly get her leg over it. That meant that Belle didn't have much choice about what to do. She took a few jerky steps after Starlight, but she didn't seem happy about it.

Stevie hurried to her horse's head. "Don't worry, Belle," she soothed her. "It's okay. We're just playing a little game of follow the leader, all right?"

She stood by Belle's head and kept her hand on the halter as Carole led Starlight forward again. This time, with Stevie to guide her, Belle seemed much more comfortable. After a few turns around the ring, Stevie stepped back.

"Try it without me this time," she said.

Carole nodded and kept Starlight moving. Belle rolled her big brown eyes in Stevie's direction, but she seemed to have figured out what was going on. She kept the lead rope taut between Starlight and herself, which made the gelding's tail look awfully funny as it stretched straight out behind him, but both horses kept going.

"Good girl!" Stevie cried in delight. She hurried forward to detach Belle from Starlight's tail and give her a congratulatory hug.

"That was great," Lisa called. "I didn't think it would work."

"Me neither," Carole said. She smiled at Stevie. "I guess Belle is a faster learner than I thought."

Stevie gave the mare a satisfied pat. "She's brilliant," she said. "I've always said so, haven't I? Come on, let's give these guys a good grooming. They deserve it."

A SHORT WHILE LATER the three girls met up again in the tack room. One of Pine Hollow's rules was that all riders were supposed to take care of the horses they rode. That included cleaning their tack after every use. Max said that having the riders pitch in was the best way to keep expenses down. But the girls knew that he also thought it was the best way to make sure his students understood that riding didn't begin when a person climbed into a saddle and end when he or she climbed out.

Luckily, cleaning tack allowed the girls to talk to each other while they worked. That meant it was usually a good time for a Saddle Club meeting.

"Okay," Carole said as she picked up a sponge. "Time to figure out what to do about New Year's Eve."

Before the other two girls could respond, a frantic voice came from the hallway outside. "Max? Are you in here?"

A second later Max's wife, Deborah, poked her head into the room.

"Oh, hi, girls," she said. She was carrying her seven-month-old baby, Maxine—already nicknamed Maxi—in an infant carrier, a sort of reverse backpack that nestled against her chest. The baby looked perfectly content to

13

be riding that way. She was smiling and sucking on a pacifier. Maxi's mother, on the other hand, looked more than a little frazzled.

"Hi, Deborah," Lisa said. "Hi, Maxi." She jumped to her feet and reached out to tickle the baby. Maxi gurgled with delight, spitting the pacifier onto the tack room floor. "Oops," Lisa said, reaching down for the pacifier. "Sorry about that."

Deborah didn't even seem to notice. "Have you seen Max lately?" she asked.

The three girls shook their heads. "Is anything wrong?" Carole asked.

Deborah sighed. "Yes. No. I don't know." She threw up her hands in exasperation. "There's a potential new riding student due to arrive here any minute. Max is supposed to be here to talk to her and check out her ability, but there's no sign of him."

"Oh," Carole said. That didn't sound like much of an emergency to her. Why was Deborah so upset? "Don't worry. I'm sure he'll turn up soon."

"I hope so," Deborah snapped. "The last thing I want to do is carry Maxi around on a stable tour. I don't think the new rider would be very impressed with that." Suddenly her voice changed from annoyed to upset. "Besides, I can't judge anyone's riding ability. I just don't know enough."

The three girls exchanged looks. Deborah seemed very

14

agitated. In fact, she was clearly on the verge of tears. And even if they didn't understand exactly why she was getting so upset about nothing, they had to try to help.

"It's okay, Deborah," Stevie said quickly. She stood up and tossed the saddle soap she was holding into the bucket by the door. "I'll go see if I can rustle up Max. Or maybe Red." Red O'Malley was the head stable hand at Pine Hollow. If Max couldn't be located, Red would be able to take over with the new student.

As Stevie rushed out the door, Carole stood, too. "I'll go tack up one of the horses," she offered. "Maybe Nero, if he's in his stall. That way he'll be all ready when the new student is ready to ride." Within seconds, she disappeared, too.

Deborah seemed slightly stunned by The Saddle Club's quick response. "Thanks, girls," she said, even though Lisa was the only one left in the room.

Lisa looked at Deborah more carefully. She could see that Deborah had black circles under her eyes. It was obvious that she was on the edge of exhaustion. Suddenly Lisa remembered that Max's mother, known to one and all as Mrs. Reg, had departed a couple of days earlier for a week's visit to friends in California. Mrs. Reg helped Max run Pine Hollow, taking care of many business matters and lots of paperwork, in addition to other stable jobs.

That must be why Deborah looks so tired, Lisa thought. *She's been doing Mrs. Reg's job around here, as well as her own job and looking after Maxi. That's a lot of work!*

"You look kind of tired," Lisa said hesitantly. "Do you want me to hold Maxi for you for a few minutes? That way you can talk to the new student in case Stevie can't find Max right away."

"Thanks, Lisa," Deborah said gratefully. "I'd appreciate that." She started to unhook the straps of the carrier. "This front pack is a miracle. It's definitely the easiest way to carry a baby, in my opinion. But Maxi is still heavier than she looks." She grinned weakly. "Max says it's because she eats like a horse."

Lisa laughed and held out her arms. Deborah slid her own arms out of the carrier and attached it around Lisa's shoulders. Lisa put her arm around the baby, who settled against the curve of her stomach.

"Neat," Lisa said, looking down at the tufts of hair on top of Maxi's head. "It's like carrying her around in a pouch, like a kangaroo."

Deborah chuckled and stretched. "It really is handy," she said. "The only drawback is that Max keeps threatening to take her on horseback in it."

Lisa laughed again. When Deborah had met Max, she had hardly known one end of a horse from the other. These days she was a little better informed. But, as she liked to put it, she still didn't eat, breathe, and sleep horses the way her husband did.

"Don't worry," Lisa joked. "We won't tease you too much if your daughter is a better rider than you are by the time she's four years old."

"That won't bother me," Deborah said with a wry smile. "In fact, I expect it. I just don't want her to be able to ride before she can walk!"

"WHERE'S THE HORSIE?" Lisa cooed. "Where's the horsie? Here's the horsie!" She pulled the stuffed toy out from behind her back and wiggled it in Maxi's face. The baby giggled and reached for the brown corduroy horse with both chubby hands. She hooked her fingers in the toy's yarn mane, and Lisa let her take it.

Lisa smiled down at Maxi. "You're awfully cute. Do you know that?" She suspected that Maxi did.

It was ten minutes since Deborah had departed to look for the new student. The other two members of The Saddle Club had not yet returned from their respective errands. Lisa was in Mrs. Reg's office playing with Maxi.

Deborah entered. "How's it going in here?" she asked.

"Great," Lisa said, looking up with a smile. "I think Maxi likes the present we got her." The stuffed horse had been a Christmas gift from The Saddle Club. Lisa had been delighted to find it tucked into the side pocket of the infant carrier.

"She sure does," Deborah said. "It's one of her favorites already. Will you come and help me welcome the new student? A car just pulled in, and I'm sure it's her."

"Sure," Lisa said. She was glad to see that Deborah seemed calmer than she had a few minutes earlier. She stood up, being careful not to bounce Maxi around too much. "Let's go."

"I really appreciate your help," Deborah said as she led the way toward the front of the building. "All of you girls, I mean. And I'm sorry if I seemed kind of hysterical before." She sighed. "I haven't been getting a lot of sleep lately. Maxi kept me up half the night last night."

Lisa glanced down at the beaming baby in her arms. She could hardly imagine such an angelic creature giving anyone trouble. "At least you won't have any problem staying awake to ring in the new year in a couple of days," she joked.

Deborah rolled her eyes. "That's true," she said with a laugh. "Who needs a party when you have a baby?" She reached over and tousled Maxi's downy hair. "She'll be our own little noisemaker this year. I just hope she lets us get more sleep in the new year than she did in the old one."

Lisa smiled. She was sure that Deborah must be exaggerating, at least a little. She knew that babies were a lot of work, but she thought that taking care of a baby must be sort of like doing stable chores. It was hard work, but you really didn't mind because it was for something you loved.

Lisa glanced again at Deborah's tired face. *Still,* she reflected, *I guess even work you love can pile up.* Sometimes completing the number of chores around Pine Hollow could seem like an impossible task. Maybe being a new mother was the same way.

She didn't have any more time to think about it. They had reached the stable entrance just in time to meet a pair of people coming through it.

One of the strangers was a girl about Lisa's age. She had short reddish brown hair, big hazel eyes, and a sprinkling of freckles across her nose. The woman with her looked so much like the girl that Lisa knew they had to be mother and daughter.

"Hi there," Deborah greeted the newcomers. "Welcome to Pine Hollow." She introduced herself and Lisa.

"Nice to meet you both," the woman said with a wide, friendly smile. She shook Deborah's hand, then turned and gave Lisa's hand a hearty shake as well. "I'm Joanne Lynn. This is my daughter, Brittney."

"Hi, Brittney," Lisa said, turning to the girl.

The new girl gave Lisa an uncertain smile. She scanned Lisa's face for a second with apparent interest, then quickly looked down at her feet. Lisa noticed that those feet were clad in a scuffed, well-worn pair of riding boots. "You can call me Britt," the girl said in a voice that was little more than a whisper.

Meanwhile, Britt's mother was leaning forward to get a better look at Maxi. "What a cute baby," she said, tickling Maxi under the chin. She glanced at Deborah. "Is she yours? I think I can see a resemblance."

Deborah smiled. "Yes, she is. Her name is Maxine. I believe you spoke to her father on the phone—Max Regnery."

"Right," Ms. Lynn said. "Max and I chatted yesterday. He sounds like a lovely man." She smiled even more brightly at Deborah, then turned to include Lisa in her frank, friendly gaze. "Britt and I just moved to this area, and she's dying to find a new stable. She's a terrific rider—she's been doing it since she was knee-high."

"Really?" Lisa said, looking at Britt. "That's great. You must be really good."

Britt shrugged. "I like to ride," she said. Then she looked down at her feet again.

The new girl seemed uncomfortable being the center of attention. Lisa could already tell that Britt was very shy. *I wonder how she turned out that way with a mother like that?* Lisa thought. Ms. Lynn was so cheerful and likable that Lisa felt comfortable with her already. Her daughter, on the other hand, seemed remote and withdrawn.

Maybe she's just timid around new people, Lisa speculated. What could Lisa do to make her feel more relaxed?

Before Lisa could figure out what to say next, Carole arrived. "Hi," she said breathlessly. "Nero's ready. He's waiting in the indoor ring."

"Thanks, Carole," Deborah said. She introduced Carole to the Lynns. "Carole and Lisa are two of our best young riders," she went on. "I'm hoping they'll help me give you two a tour of the place." She gave Ms. Lynn an apologetic smile. "I'm afraid I can't seem to locate my husband at the moment. But he'll be along soon, I'm sure."

"No problem," Ms. Lynn said. "We're in no hurry. Right, Britt?"

Britt nodded silently.

"Great. How about that tour?" Ms. Lynn turned her bright smile and twinkling hazel eyes on Carole, who automatically grinned back.

"Let's start at the tack room," Carole said. "Come this way." She touched Britt on the elbow. The girl jumped in surprise, but she followed obediently as Carole led the way down the hall, pointing things out as they walked.

Lisa dropped behind a little, watching Britt. She could tell that the girl wasn't doing much more chatting with Carole than she had with her. But she did seem very interested in seeing the stable. She even asked Carole a question or two, although she spoke so quietly that Lisa couldn't quite make out what she was asking.

After a moment, Ms. Lynn fell into step beside Lisa. "Have you been riding here long, Lisa?" she asked.

"Not as long as my friends have," Lisa said. She looked around at the familiar scene. It was hard to remember a time when she hadn't come here, although it really wasn't that far in the past. "But long enough to know that this is the best stable around. I'm sure Britt will love it here."

"I hope so," Ms. Lynn said. Her smile turned a little wistful and she lowered her voice. "In case you haven't noticed, she's a little shy. But only with people, never with horses. She loves them all." The woman glanced down one of the long rows of stalls as they passed it. "She must get that from my late husband. She sure doesn't get it from me. I never even saw a horse up close before Britt started taking lessons."

Lisa laughed as she and Ms. Lynn paused outside the tack room. Carole, Britt, and Deborah had already disappeared inside. "Don't worry, the horses here are really friendly," Lisa assured the woman. "And the people are almost as nice." Maxi wiggled a little in the carrier, and Lisa helped the baby find a more comfortable position as Ms. Lynn peeked into the tack room. Lisa could hear the sounds of one of Carole's enthusiastic horse-related lectures heating up inside.

Ms. Lynn pulled her head back and looked at Lisa. "Sounds like they're having fun in there."

"I'm sure Carole is," Lisa said. "I just hope she doesn't get so caught up in what she's saying that she won't let Britt get a word in edgewise. She gets that way sometimes when the subject is horses."

Ms. Lynn laughed. "Don't worry," she assured Lisa, leaning back against the hallway wall. "Britt is a good listener. She could listen to horse talk all day and be as happy as a clam." Maxi reached out toward the woman, and Ms. Lynn offered the baby a finger to grasp. "Do you go to school here in Willow Creek, Lisa?"

Lisa nodded. "I go to the public school in town."

"That's where Britt will be going when classes start up again in January." Ms. Lynn shook her head. "I really hated to pull her out of her old school in Ohio in the middle of the year, but I didn't have much choice. I work for a politician who was just elected to Congress in November. She asked me to move here and work for her; her term starts this January."

"That's really great," Lisa said sincerely. Willow Creek was within commuting distance of Washington, D.C., so she knew a lot of people, including many of her parents' friends and a few of Max's adult riders, who worked for the government in one capacity or another. She was always interested in meeting the people who had moved to the U.S. capital from all over the country—even all over

24

the world. It made her sleepy little town seem much more exciting.

"This way," Carole called over her shoulder, hurrying out of the tack room. She almost bumped into Lisa. "Oops. Sorry about that. I was just going to take Britt to meet some of the horses."

"Good idea," Lisa agreed. She smiled at Ms. Lynn as Carole hurried off with Britt in tow. "Nobody knows the horses around here better than Carole. Just don't tell Max I said so."

The woman chuckled. Deborah, who had just emerged from the tack room and joined them, laughed, too. "I'm afraid Lisa is right about that," she admitted. "Carole is certifiably horse-crazy."

"The best kind of crazy," Ms. Lynn said. "At least that's what Britt tells me."

Lisa glanced down the hallway at Britt's departing back. The more she heard about the new girl, the better she liked her. At least in theory. It was just too bad that Britt wasn't as friendly and outgoing as her mother.

"What kinds of horses did Britt ride at her old stable?" Deborah asked as she, Lisa, and Ms. Lynn strolled down the hallway after Carole and Britt.

"Actually, she had her own horse," Ms. Lynn replied. "His name is Toledo. She boarded him at the stable. Unfortunately, he was already quite old when she got him a few years ago." She glanced forward at her daughter's back. "We decided to let him retire and stay in Ohio rather than trying to move him here with us. He's got a beautiful little pasture at the stable there. But Britt misses him terribly already, as you can imagine."

Lisa nodded sympathetically. She couldn't imagine leaving a beloved horse behind in another state. But it sounded as though Britt had made her decision based on what was best for her horse. That was another big point in her favor, in Lisa's book. She was sure her friends would agree. "That's tough," she said softly.

Deborah nodded. "Poor girl. I hope we can help keep her busy so that she doesn't feel too sad."

At that moment, Britt came hurrying back toward them. "Hey, Mom," she said. Her voice was still soft and quick, but now she was smiling. Her face glowed with excitement. "Come here and see. There's a horse here who looks a lot like Toledo."

Ms. Lynn allowed herself to be dragged away down the aisle. Carole walked over to talk to Lisa while Deborah wandered around the corner to look for Max.

"Which horse is it?" Lisa asked curiously.

"Romeo," Carole said.

Lisa nodded. Romeo was a boarder. He was a good-natured brown gelding that belonged to Polly Giacomin, a girl in The Saddle Club's riding class. "Britt seems nice, doesn't she?"

"Nice and shy," Carole agreed. "But she seems to know a lot about horses."

26

Lisa smiled. She knew that was all the endorsement Carole needed. "Did she tell you about her old horse?"

"Not very much," Carole said. "What's the story?"

Lisa told her what she knew. She had hardly finished when she heard a voice behind them.

"Here we are!" Stevie announced. She barreled around the corner, pulling Max along behind her by the arm.

Carole and Lisa hurried to meet them. "Where were you?" Carole asked Max.

Max gave her a glance that was halfway between amused and annoyed. "Do I work for you three now?" he asked. "When was the coup?"

Stevie rolled her eyes. "It's a good thing we're here," she told him. "Otherwise your wife would have gone crazy and your new student would have wandered off to another stable before you ever got back."

Maxi spotted her father and stretched out her arms toward him, babbling.

"I see you've kidnapped my child, too," Max said, letting the baby grab on to his fingers. "What have you done with Deborah?"

"Max!" Deborah cried, rounding the corner. "Thank goodness Stevie found you." She dragged him off in the direction the Lynns had gone. "Can you watch the baby for a few more minutes?" she called over her shoulder.

"No problem," Lisa called after her. She turned to Stevie. "Where did you find him?"

Stevie waved one hand uninterestedly. "Oh, he and Red were having some kind of debate with the grain delivery guy," she said. "But that's not important now. What's the story with the new girl? Is she our age? Is she nice? Can she ride?"

"Let's go see for ourselves," Carole said, answering the last question first. "Max is supposed to watch her ride right now."

The three girls hurried to the indoor ring. They arrived just behind Max, Britt, and the others.

"I hope Britt doesn't get nervous with all of us watching her," Lisa said.

But the new girl hardly seemed to notice their presence. She walked up to Nero, one of the oldest and steadiest mounts in the stable. He had been trained by Max's father and was always a safe choice for a new rider.

As soon as Britt was in the saddle, The Saddle Club could tell that she could have handled a much more spirited horse. She mounted easily with a boost from Max, took the reins with confidence, and soon had Nero trotting around the ring. She touched him with her boot, and he broke into a lumbering but enthusiastic canter.

"Wow," Carole said. "I can't remember the last time I saw Nero canter."

"I don't think I've ever seen him canter," Lisa said. "Britt's good, isn't she?"

Stevie nodded, looking impressed. "She makes old

Nero seem like a lively young thing," she said. "No easy task there."

As Britt continued her ride, with Max watching carefully, Ms. Lynn came over to The Saddle Club. Lisa and Carole introduced her to Stevie.

"Britt really seems to like it here," the woman said happily. "I was afraid we would have to try out a few stables before she found the right one."

"Don't be silly," Stevie said quickly. "This is the best—the *only*—choice in the whole area."

Lisa laughed. "You'd better not let Phil hear you say that, Stevie," she teased. Phil rode at a stable called Cross County, which sometimes competed against Pine Hollow at Pony Club rallies.

"Or the people at Hedgerow," Carole added. Hedgerow Farms was another nearby stable. Max was friends with the manager there, a woman named Elaine, and The Saddle Club knew that Hedgerow was a lovely, well-run establishment.

"Seriously, though," Lisa told Ms. Lynn. "I'm sure Britt will be happy here. Maybe she'll find a horse she likes almost as much as Toledo."

The woman glanced over at her daughter, who was still mounted on Nero. Britt had pulled the old horse to a halt and was nodding as Max talked to her. "Actually, I wanted to talk to you girls about that," Ms. Lynn said quietly. "I want to get Britt a new horse. It won't replace

Toledo in her heart, but I can tell she really wants one."
She grinned mischievously. "Somehow, though, she's
gotten it in her head that we don't have enough money
right now because of the move, so she won't just come
right out and ask me about getting a new horse. My Britt
is anything but selfish. That's why I want to surprise her if
I can."

"Are you sure that's a good idea?" Carole said quickly.
"If she's going to ride the horse, she should be the one to
pick it out. Otherwise—"

Ms. Lynn cut her off. "I know, I know," she said with a
smile. "Believe me, I haven't lived with my daughter all
these years without picking up a little bit of horse sense.
But if I can, I'd like her to pick out her next horse without realizing that's what she's doing. If you know what I
mean."

Carole and Lisa looked a little confused, but Stevie
nodded immediately. "I get it," she said. "But I think
you're going to need some help."

Ms. Lynn smiled at Stevie hopefully. "I know," she
said. "And I know I just met you three, but . . ."

"Say no more," Stevie said. "The Saddle Club is on
the case."

Now it was Ms. Lynn's turn to look confused. The girls
quickly explained what The Saddle Club was. And they
all promised to help track down promising horses that
were for sale.

"We can just happen to arrange for her to ride a bunch

30

of different horses and see how she likes them," Stevie explained to her friends.

"Oh, I see," Lisa said as she caught on. "It makes perfect sense. A rider who's new to the stable ought to try a number of horses anyway, right?"

"Right," Carole confirmed. "It sounds like fun." She smiled at Ms. Lynn. "Don't worry. With us on the job, Britt will have the perfect horse in no time."

"Great," Ms. Lynn said, smiling back. "I'd love to help her find a horse before the vacation is over. I think it would make it easier for her to start in her new school."

Lisa knew that the woman's logic probably wouldn't make sense to some people. What did having a horse have to do with going to school? But she herself had no trouble understanding exactly what Ms. Lynn meant. "We'll do whatever we can," she promised.

"Thank you so much," the woman said. "I just know this will be the best holiday present Britt could have."

They had to change the subject after that because Britt had dismounted and was walking toward them. Max and Deborah were right behind her.

"What do you think, honey?" Ms. Lynn asked. "Do you want to give Pine Hollow a try?"

Britt nodded. She still didn't seem to have much to say, but now she was definitely smiling.

"I was just telling your daughter," Max said to Ms. Lynn, "that what we can do, if you like, is have Britt start coming here on a trial basis for a few weeks. Sort of a guest membership, if you will. That way she'll be able to get a better idea of what this place is all about."

"Wonderful," Ms. Lynn said. She put an arm around Britt's shoulders and squeezed her tightly. "I'm sure she'll love it here. Right, honey?"

Britt blushed and looked a little embarrassed. But she also looked happy.

Carole felt happy, too. She loved meeting people who loved horses as much as she did. And even though Britt hadn't been terribly friendly today, Carole was sure she would loosen up once she started coming to Pine Hollow regularly. The Saddle Club would see to that.

Besides, it would be a lot of fun to help Ms. Lynn find Britt the perfect horse. That kind of project was right up The Saddle Club's alley!

Ms. Lynn gave the three girls a wink as she and Britt said good-bye and got ready to leave. "I'll be in touch," she whispered as she passed Carole. When Britt wasn't looking, the woman tucked a small piece of paper into Carole's hand.

Carole looked down. It was a business card with Ms. Lynn's phone number on it. "I guess she's serious about wanting our help," she said, showing it to her friends after the Lynns had gone.

"She'd better be," Stevie said, rubbing her hands together eagerly. "Because we're on the case now."

As Max started walking around the ring with Nero to

cool him down, Deborah came over to the girls. "Thanks again for everything," she told them. "I know Max appreciates it, too. I can take Maxi back now."

Lisa gave the baby a quick hug before unfastening the carrier. "I hate to give her up," she said. "She's been a perfect angel. I think she really likes it in the stable."

Deborah rolled her eyes, and the girls laughed. "Don't fight it, Deborah," Stevie advised her with a twinkle in her eye. "Maxi was born to be in a barn. It's in her blood." Max wasn't the first one in his family to run Pine Hollow. His father had done it before him, and his grandfather had started the place. The Saddle Club was sure that Maxi was destined to be the next Regnery to take over the family business.

"Maybe I should try letting her sleep in a stall," Deborah said. "She might let me get some rest that way." She gave the girls a quick wave and walked out of the ring.

"She was joking about that stall thing, wasn't she?" Carole said.

Stevie shrugged. "It was hard to tell," she said with a grin. "Who knows—maybe it would work. Maxi *is* a Regnery, after all. But enough about Deborah. We've got a Saddle Club project to work on, remember? We've got to find Britt a horse."

Carole nodded and led the way out of the ring. The girls paused in the hallway just outside. "I know a few places I can call," Carole said. She sometimes volunteered as an assistant to Judy Barker, the local equine vet. Judy visited most of the horse farms in the area on her rounds.

"We should definitely check at Hedgerow," Stevie suggested. "And I'll have Phil ask around at Cross County when he gets back from his vacation."

Lisa was only half listening to her friends. She was still thinking about their previous topic. "I think Deborah is working too hard," she said suddenly.

Her friends turned to stare at her. "What?" Stevie said.

Lisa told them what she had been thinking. "Deborah seems really tired. Not only does she have to take care of Maxi and keep up with her job at the newspaper, but she's also pitching in more around here this week while Mrs. Reg is away. I think it's really getting to her. And I don't think she and Max are even planning to go out on New Year's Eve."

"So what are you saying?" Carole asked.

Lisa leaned against the stable wall. "Isn't it obvious? Deborah needs a break. Max does, too, for that matter. You know he hardly ever takes any time off."

"You're not thinking about staging that coup Max was talking about, are you?" Stevie asked with a grin.

Lisa laughed. "No way," she said. "But I do have an idea. All this talk about holiday gifts—you know, Britt's new horse—made me realize something. We gave Maxi a present this year, but we didn't give Max and Deborah anything."

"You're right," Carole said. She shrugged and picked at a splinter on the wall she was leaning against. "I guess maybe we should have. But Maxi's stuffed pony used up all our money, and I'm sure Max and Deborah didn't really expect anything from us. Anyway, I'm still not sure what you're driving at, Lisa."

Lisa sighed. "Isn't it obvious?" she said again. "The perfect gift for Deborah and Max is right in front of our noses—"

She bit off her next words when Max emerged from the indoor ring with Nero strolling sedately behind him.

"I'll tell you later," Lisa whispered to her friends.

Max spotted the three girls and asked, "What is this, a tea party? What are you girls doing standing around chatting? Didn't I see a pile of dirty saddles in the tack room?"

Stevie's eyes widened. "How does he do that?" she said wonderingly as Max continued on his way. The girls scurried back to their unfinished cleaning task. "I was with him on our way back here, remember? And we didn't go anywhere near the tack room!"

"CAN I RESERVE another table for two?" Colonel Hanson said into the phone. He paused, listening to the person on the other end of the line. Carole held her breath and crossed her fingers.

A moment later, her father gave her a wink and a thumbs-up sign. "Great," he told the person on the phone. "Thank you very much. The name is Regnery. They'll be there at seven-fifteen."

He hung up the phone and grinned. "Okay, sweetheart," he told Carole. "Max and Deborah have a reservation for New Year's Eve. Whether they want one or not."

"They want one," Carole assured him, giving him a

quick thank-you hug. "Or they will, once we get through with them."

Colonel Hanson laughed. "Somehow I have no trouble believing that," he said. He grinned. "And don't worry—Linda and I will keep an eye on them for you. We'll make sure they're having fun."

Linda was Colonel Hanson's date for New Year's Eve. The two of them were going to the same New Year's Eve dinner theater in Washington, D.C., where Max and Deborah now had reservations. All the couples would be served a gourmet meal, then see a stage show, and then end the evening with a special celebration and dancing at midnight.

Colonel Hanson went into the living room and sank into his favorite chair. Carole perched on the arm of the couch next to him. "I can't wait to see their faces when we tell them," she said eagerly.

"I'm sure they'll be thrilled," her father said. "Having a baby is wonderful, but sometimes it can be just as wonderful to get away and talk to other adults for an evening." He grinned and winked. "Not that your mom and I ever felt that way about *you*, of course."

Carole stuck out her tongue at him playfully. "I certainly hope not," she said.

"So whose idea was this plot, anyway?" Colonel Hanson asked. "No, don't tell me. Let me guess. This has the look of a Stevie Lake scheme."

"Guess again," Carole said. "Lisa came up with the idea."

Colonel Hanson put his hands behind his head and stretched out more comfortably. "Lisa? Well, I guess I shouldn't be surprised," he said. "All three of you girls manage to come up with some pretty interesting ideas when you get together."

AT HER HOUSE, Lisa was thinking the same thing. She was sitting in front of her family's computer, working in a greeting-card design program.

She tilted her head and looked critically at the image on the screen. *Happy Holidays, Max and Deborah*, the card read in curly script. *From The Saddle Club.*

Below that, the card continued:

We know that new parents don't have much time to make plans. So we've made them for you. You are invited to a wonderful New Year's Eve of dining and dancing the night away. In addition, we are happy to provide baby-sitting services for the entire evening. And all we expect in return is free access to your refrigerator!

That last line had been Stevie's idea. Lisa giggled as she read it.

The card looked good. Lisa nodded with satisfaction and typed one more line at the bottom in smaller print:

All non-baby-related expenses to be assumed by the recipients.

That had been Stevie's idea, too. Lisa wasn't sure whether it came from Stevie's sense of humor or from the fact that both her parents were lawyers. But she decided it didn't matter. She was sure Max and Deborah would be amused, and that was all that counted.

Lisa hit Save, then Print. She sat back and waited for the card to emerge from the printer.

She was still proud of herself for realizing that Max and Deborah needed an evening to themselves. They had both been a bit moody and irritable lately, and Lisa was sure it was because they were working too hard. They needed to get away from all their responsibilities for a while and just concentrate on having a good time.

And The Saddle Club was going to make sure it happened. Carole and Stevie had immediately been enthusiastic about Lisa's idea to give the Regnerys a free night of baby-sitting on New Year's Eve. And both of them had added their own ideas, making it even better. Carole had suggested making reservations at the place in Washington. That way, it would be harder for Max and Deborah to make excuses not to go. And it had been Stevie's idea to surprise the couple with a card—though she had been happy to let Lisa, the most artistic member of the group, design it.

It had also been Stevie who had pointed out that this

was the perfect solution to their own New Year's Eve dilemma as well. Now they could have their sleepover at Max and Deborah's big, rambling farmhouse, without worrying about parents or brothers getting in the way of their fun. The only person they would have to share the place with would be Maxi, and they didn't mind that one bit.

Lisa smiled as she thought about it. They could start out the evening by playing with the baby. Then, when Maxi had fallen asleep, The Saddle Club could move on to the rest of their plans—making resolutions, playing games, talking about their newest Saddle Club project. And, according to Stevie, making prank phone calls to a certain local New Year's Eve party . . .

It would be great. What could be better than a night-long Saddle Club meeting free of distractions?

AT THAT MOMENT, Stevie was feeling more than a little distracted. That was because she was talking on the phone to Phil and fighting off her brothers at the same time.

"So what do you think you'll be doing on New Year's Eve at mid— Oof! Wait a second," Stevie said into the phone.

She tucked the receiver under her arm and grabbed the soccer ball that had just hit her in the stomach. She crouched down behind the kitchen counter, holding the ball ready.

After a moment, a grinning face peered around the corner of the door frame. It was her twin brother, Alex.

Stevie didn't hesitate. She took aim and fired. Her brother pulled his head back just in time, and the ball bounced off the wall in the hallway outside the door. A pair of hands reached out and snatched it out of Stevie's sight.

Stevie sighed and put the phone back to her ear, doing her best to ignore her younger brother, Michael, who had his face pressed to the glass outside the kitchen window. She couldn't hear him from inside, but she could tell what he was doing. He was making smooching sounds against the window.

"I hope your lips get stuck," she muttered in his general direction.

She couldn't believe he was braving the icy cold evening air just to annoy her. There were a couple of inches of snow on the ground, and the wind was wailing around the eaves of the house, making Stevie feel cold just listening to it. But on second thought, she figured she shouldn't be surprised. Her brothers were a lot like the U.S. Postal Service that way. Neither snow nor rain nor heat nor gloom of night could stop them from torturing her every chance they got.

"I guess I should have taken this call in my room," Stevie told Phil. She had a phone on the table beside her bed, but she had been in the kitchen when Phil had called, and she hadn't wanted to waste any time running upstairs. After all, Phil was leaving first thing the next morning.

Phil laughed on the other end of the line. One of the best things about him, as far as Stevie was concerned, was that he really understood how annoying her brothers could be. He had three sisters who drove him equally crazy.

"In answer to the question you were asking before you were so rudely interrupted," he said, "I hope I'll be talking to you at midnight on New Year's Eve. Even if it's only on the phone."

Stevie beamed. "Really?" she said. "That would be great. I didn't even think about that. We should definitely call each other at midnight."

"I have an even better idea," Phil said. "Let's call each other every hour on the hour. That way it will almost seem like we're spending the whole evening together like we wanted to."

Out of the corner of her eye, Stevie noticed that Michael had disappeared from the window. But she didn't care. She was too excited about what Phil had said. "What a fantastic idea!" she exclaimed. "Like I told you, I'll be baby-sitting at Max and Deborah's all night. So I'll have plenty of time to talk. Carole and Lisa won't mind."

"Great," Phil said. "I'll just have to make sure I'm at the hotel at the right time. But that will be no problem. If my family doesn't want to come back with me from wherever we are, I can just take the monorail back by myself."

Stevie couldn't help sighing at that. She was still disappointed that she wouldn't be going to Disney World herself. Riding the monorail and doing all kinds of other fun stuff with Phil would be the best way to welcome in the New Year, bar none. But she would have to settle for what she could get.

"It's a deal," she said. "I'll get my parents to lend me their calling card so that Max and Deborah won't get charged for the long-distance calls. I can use some of my Christmas money to pay off the card."

"Good," Phil said. "And we can take turns calling each other and share the expenses."

Stevie was about to say something else, but suddenly she felt something hit the back of her head with a loud, wet *whap!* Before she could react, icy rivulets started snaking their way down her neck to her back.

Glancing at the floor, she saw a large snowball that was already starting to melt into a puddle. She whirled around. *"Hey!"* she shouted at her brothers at the top of her lungs. All three of them were standing in the kitchen doorway, laughing their heads off. Michael was brushing snow off his mittens.

"Ow!" Phil protested in her ear.

Stevie realized she had forgotten to move the receiver before yelling at her brothers. "Oops," she told Phil.

"Sorry. I think I'd better go. I have a little something to take care of here." She glared at her brothers. They grinned and took off.

"I understand," Phil said with a laugh. "I've got to get going, too. I still have some packing to do. But I'll call you New Year's Eve. Shall we say six o'clock?"

"I'll be waiting by the phone," Stevie promised.

THE NEXT MORNING, the three girls arrived at the foot of Pine Hollow's gravel driveway at the same time. They greeted each other, then hurried into the stable building together. They were eager to find Max and Deborah and present their gift. But when they entered, they saw that Max already had his hands full.

"I'll be with you in just a second, Mr. French," he was calling to one of his adult riders, who was waiting patiently to talk to him. Meanwhile, Max was leading a horse named Barq with one hand and another stable horse, Coconut, with the other. Maxi was bouncing along happily in the infant carrier, which was buckled over Max's shoulders.

Carole noticed another man hurrying forward to help. She recognized Alec McAllister, the blacksmith Max generally used to shoe his horses.

"Hey there, girls," Alec greeted The Saddle Club cheerfully.

"Hi," Carole greeted the redheaded young man. "What are you doing here today?" The blacksmith's regular monthly visit to Pine Hollow wasn't for at least a week.

Max answered for the blacksmith. "He's here because Barq decided to throw a shoe this morning," he grumbled, giving the lively Arabian gelding a dirty look. "As if I didn't have enough to do around here already."

The three girls exchanged looks. Max almost never blamed his horses for his own workload, no matter what they did. He knew better than anyone what came with running a stable. From the sound of things, their gift was coming just in the nick of time for him as well as for Deborah.

"Let me hold Coconut while Alec gets started," Lisa offered, stepping forward.

Max gladly relinquished the horse's lead line. Lisa took it and stroked Coconut's soft nose.

"Did Coconut throw a shoe, too?" she asked.

Alec gestured to the gelding's feet. "Take a look," he said.

At that moment Coconut shifted his weight, and the girls could see that he had no shoes on any of his feet. They knew that Max, like most good horsemen, liked to let each of his horses go shoeless for at least a couple of weeks each year. It was a good way to make sure their feet stayed as healthy as possible.

"As long as I was coming, Max decided we might as well put Coconut's shoes back on," Alec said. "He's had enough of a vacation."

Lisa smoothed the friendly horse's straw-colored mane. Coconut was a flaxen chestnut, which meant his mane and tail were a slightly lighter color than his golden yellow body. "Did you hear that, boy?" she said. "It's back to work for you. I bet you're looking forward to that, huh?" She had never ridden Coconut, but Carole had told her that he was among the best-behaved horses in the stable.

For his part, Max was behaving very strangely at the moment. He had been paying no attention to the girls' conversation with the blacksmith. In fact, he didn't even seem to remember where he was or what he was supposed to be doing. He raised both hands and rubbed his forehead until his hair stood straight up. Even Maxi gave him a funny look.

"Are you okay, Max?" Stevie asked worriedly.

Max didn't seem to hear the question. He started looking back and forth between Alec, who had set to work on Barq's foot, and the hallway leading to the tack room and Mrs. Reg's office. "I should go help Deborah," he muttered uncertainly. "But I should help Red bring down the hay. And I should check the other horses' feet while Alec is here."

"Um, Max?" Carole said. "We'll help out if you want. What's Deborah doing?"

Max looked straight at the girls for the first time. "Oh, hello," he said. "When did you get here?"

"Uh-oh," Stevie murmured. "There's no time to waste. This is an emergency."

46

Her friends knew exactly what she meant.

Lisa quickly put Coconut in cross-ties in a nearby aisle so that he'd be ready when Alec finished with Barq. Meanwhile, Carole and Stevie each took Max firmly by an elbow.

"Now," Stevie said, "let's try this again. Where's Deborah?"

Max stared down at the girls' hands on his arms, looking slightly confused, but he didn't comment. "She's in the office," he said instead. "Answering the phone. It's been ringing off the hook all morning."

"Okay. Now we're getting somewhere," Stevie said.

Before Max knew what was happening, Stevie and Carole had steered him down the aisle and into Mrs. Reg's office. Lisa followed, shutting the office door behind her. Deborah was sitting behind the desk. As they entered, she was just hanging up the phone, shaking her head.

"Whew," she said. "I can't believe so many people suddenly have urgent questions two days before New Year's Eve. Haven't they ever heard of taking a holiday?" She stood up and walked around the desk, reaching out for Maxi.

Max handed over the baby. "Do you mind taking her for a while? I've got to take care of the hay, and—"

"Not quite yet," Stevie interrupted. She waited until Maxi was safe in her mother's arms, then continued. "We have something to say to you."

Lisa reached into her coat pocket and pulled out the envelope containing the card she had made the night before. She handed it to Stevie.

Carole held her breath as she waited to see the presentation. Despite all their careful planning, she felt a little nervous. What if Max and Deborah turned down their gift? They were both so responsible. They might decide they ought to stay at home and take care of things there instead of going out and having fun.

One glance at the determined expression on Stevie's face reassured Carole a little bit. The girls had already vowed that they weren't going to take no for an answer. Even if Max and Deborah resisted the idea at first, The Saddle Club would just have to talk them into it. They would do whatever it took to make sure the couple had some nice, relaxing, romantic, adults-only time together.

Deborah was back in her seat, holding Maxi in one arm while scrabbling around on Mrs. Reg's desk with the other. The desk, which Max's mother usually kept in a sort of disorderly order, was just plain disorderly now. It was covered with documents, sales bills and invoices, and miscellaneous scraps of paper.

"There was an urgent message for you here somewhere from that tack company . . . ," Deborah told Max anxiously.

Maxi chose that moment to spit her pacifier onto the floor. She peered down after it with a surprised expression on her chubby face. Then she opened her mouth and started to wail.

Max let out a sigh and hurried forward to grab the baby. He put her over his shoulder and patted her gently on the back while Deborah picked up the pacifier and rushed to the tack room next door. Over Maxi's cries, the girls could hear the sound of running water as Deborah rinsed it in the small sink there.

A moment later all was well again, at least with Maxi. She sucked contentedly on the pacifier while Deborah rocked her in both arms. Maxi's parents, on the other hand, looked more weary and frazzled than ever.

Stevie stopped Max as he was about to rush out of the room to find Red. "Just one second," she said. "I know you're both busy. And we'll be happy to pitch in with the chores as soon as we've finished here." She nodded toward her friends.

"Great," Max said. "In that case, Carole and Lisa, can you give all the horses' feet a quick check before Alex leaves? And Stevie, could you muck out Coconut's and Barq's stalls while they're—"

"Hold it." Stevie's voice took on a no-nonsense tone that sounded an awful lot like Max's own when the instructor had something important to say. Carole could hardly keep from laughing at the startled expression on Max's face. Deborah looked just as surprised. Even Maxi looked at Stevie with interest.

"What is it, Stevie?" Deborah asked.

Stevie held out the envelope. "We have something for you two," she said. "It's sort of a Christmas present. Well, more of a New Year's Eve present, really. Let's just call it a holiday present."

"For us?" Max took the envelope, looking mystified. He slit it open with his thumb and pulled out the card.

"What is it, Max?" Deborah asked curiously.

He walked over to her, reading the card as he did. Carole couldn't read the expression on his face. "Look at this," he told his wife. "The girls want to baby-sit for us on New Year's Eve while we go out."

"We made reservations for you and everything," Lisa said in a rush. "And we'll come to your house and watch Maxi the whole time you're gone. You won't have to do a thing except drive yourself to the restaurant in Washington." She smiled sheepishly. "And pay the bill, of course."

"Hmm," Max said. He gazed at Deborah. She gazed back silently.

Carole bit her lip. She couldn't stand the suspense. After all The Saddle Club had done, were Max and Deborah going to say no?

Stevie obviously thought so. "Listen," she said, "I don't care what arguments you have against this. We think—"

Max and Deborah didn't let her finish. They both spoke up at once. "We'll take it!" they said quickly.

". . . AND I MISS YOU, too," Stevie said. "I'll talk to you in an hour." She hung up the phone.

It was shortly after six P.M. on New Year's Eve. Stevie and Phil had just completed the first of their hourly phone calls. They were careful to keep the call to just a few minutes so that their parents wouldn't get upset about the long-distance charges. But it was better than nothing, Stevie reminded herself.

She glanced at her watch. It had stopped at four-thirty that morning. "It's a good thing Phil offered to make the first call," she muttered. She hurried into the kitchen and checked the clock on the microwave oven. She set and wound her watch, then went out to the front hall, where her overnight bag and sleeping bag were waiting.

Opening the hall closet, Stevie started to grab her warmest down coat. It was colder than ever that night, and even though Pine Hollow was only a short walk away, Stevie knew she would need to bundle up.

But her hand paused inches from the coat. She had just spotted something else in the closet. It was Phil's favorite pro sports team jacket. He had left it at Stevie's house one day about a month ago, and she'd forgotten to return it. Seeing it hanging there suddenly made her miss Phil more than ever. Florida seemed very far away.

On an impulse, Stevie pulled the bright green-and-yellow jacket off its hanger and slipped it on. It was a bit big on her, but she liked the way it felt. It wasn't nearly as warm as her other coat, but she decided that didn't matter. She wouldn't be spending much time outdoors tonight. And this would be one more way of helping her pretend that she and Phil were spending the holiday together.

The buzzing of the doorbell interrupted her thoughts. "Uh-oh," she muttered. "The invasion of the creeps is starting."

Chad raced into the hall and shoved past her to get to the door. "I thought you were leaving," he tossed back over his shoulder as he swung the door open.

"Don't worry," Stevie said. She stood to one side as

several members of Chad's soccer team jostled their way inside, complaining about the cold. "I was just on my way out." She slung her bag over her shoulder and hurried through the door a split second before Chad slammed it shut.

Stevie almost turned back for her warm jacket when she felt the first blast of icy wind hit her. But she couldn't stand the thought of going back inside with Chad and his buddies. She wrapped her arms around herself and broke into a jog to keep warm as she headed down the driveway and turned in the direction of Pine Hollow.

As she hurried along the streets that separated her house from the stable, Stevie thought about the evening ahead. She couldn't wait to start The Saddle Club's official New Year's Eve sleepover. She couldn't wait to talk about Britt and her surprise horse. She couldn't wait to talk to Phil on the phone. Her cold face broke into a mischievous grin. She also couldn't wait to start making prank calls to her brother's party. Ideas were already percolating in her mind.

Before long, the familiar buildings of Pine Hollow came into view. Stevie put on an extra burst of speed. Max and Deborah's house was on a hill beyond the stable, but Stevie figured she had a few minutes before she had to be there. First she would stop in to wish Belle a happy New Year.

She swung open the door and sighed in relief as the

warm, heated air inside the stable met her. Closing the door carefully behind her, she dropped her things against the wall and walked toward Belle's stall.

Halfway there, she ran into Max. He was still wearing his work clothes—a pair of dusty jeans and a worn flannel shirt.

"I hope you're not planning to wear that to the restaurant tonight," Stevie said.

Max glanced at his watch. "At this rate, I'm not sure I'll be able to go tonight."

Stevie's jaw dropped. "What!" she exclaimed. "You've got to be kidding."

Max's face looked set and anxious. "What can I do?" he said. "Joanne Lynn was supposed to stop by and drop off a check for Britt's first few lessons. But she hasn't shown up yet."

"And?" Stevie prompted him.

Max shrugged. "And nothing," he said. "Isn't that enough? I can't reach her on the phone, and Red has already left for the night. And in weather like this, I'd hate to think of her driving all the way out here and—"

Stevie didn't let him finish. "Don't be ridiculous," she said firmly. She hurried back down the aisle to the entrance. Unzipping her overnight bag, she dug through its contents. Soon she found what she was looking for—a pen and a pad of paper.

"Watch this," she said.

In large letters, she wrote, "Ms. Lynn: When you get here, please come to the house up the hill."

She held it up for Max to see. "Okay?" she said. "I think she can handle that. And I think Carole, Lisa, and I can handle taking a check for you."

Max stared at the note for a moment. Then he smiled. "I guess you can," he admitted, rubbing his eyes. "Sorry. I must be more tired than I thought."

"That's why you need to get up to the house and change clothes right now," Stevie said, shooing him toward the door. "You need to relax for at least one evening. And so does your wife. Now scoot. Or we may decide to spend Ms. Lynn's check ourselves, just to teach you a lesson."

Max gave her a dirty look, but he grabbed his coat and raced out of the building without another word.

He had hardly left when the door opened again, letting in another cold blast of wind. Carole and Lisa hurried through the doorway.

"Brrr! It's cold out there!" Lisa exclaimed.

Carole smiled when she saw Stevie. "There you are," she said. "I called your house to see if you wanted a ride. Dad drove me here, and he stopped to pick up Lisa on the way. Chad said you'd already left. He sounded pretty happy about it, too."

Stevie rolled her eyes. "That's exactly why I was in such a hurry to get out of there," she said. "But never mind that." She quickly filled her friends in on her recent encounter with Max.

Lisa turned to Carole. "See? I told you I saw someone running up the hill."

"I couldn't tell," Carole said. "My eyeballs were frozen just walking here from the car." She looked at her watch. "I want to check on Starlight before we go up to the house, okay?"

"My thoughts exactly," Stevie agreed.

A few minutes later, satisfied that their horses were warm and comfortable, the girls left the stable, and Lisa and Carole raced across the grassy, tree-dotted lawn that lay between them and the Regnery home. Stevie paused just long enough to attach her note firmly to the latch outside the stable door. She checked to make sure it wouldn't blow away, then ran after her friends. She caught up just as they jumped the three steps leading to the porch and rang the bell.

The door flew open within seconds. "Come on in," Deborah greeted them. "You must be frozen."

The girls obeyed. They set their bags down and stared at Deborah.

"Wow," Carole said.

"Ditto," Stevie agreed, and Lisa nodded.

Deborah looked beautiful. She was wearing a silky chocolate brown dress, and her hair was swept up on top of her head. She had applied just enough subtle makeup to flatter her even features and clear, pale skin.

"Thanks," Deborah said, smiling at them. She looked more relaxed than Carole could remember her looking in months. "Come on in. Maxi is in the living room in her playpen."

Max came down the stairs as the girls followed Deborah into the living room. His hair was damp and he was still knotting his tie. But he, too, looked more relaxed and festive already.

He smiled at The Saddle Club. "Just in time," he said. He slipped an arm around Deborah's waist and gave her a quick kiss on the cheek. "Ready? We'd better get going or we'll be late."

Deborah nodded. She went to the playpen, where Maxi was sucking on one of her stuffed horse's ears. "Good-bye, sweetie," she crooned. She grabbed the baby and picked her up, hugging her tight. "You'll be good for the girls, won't you, Maxi?"

"I'm sure she will," Lisa said. "Don't worry about a thing. Just have a good time." She slipped off her coat and reached for the baby.

Deborah reluctantly handed her over. "Okay," she said. "But if you have any problems, the number of the restaurant is stuck to the refrigerator. I also wrote it on the pad by the upstairs phone, just in case. The doctor's number is there, too, and the poison control center's number, and—"

"We know, we know," Stevie said, giving Deborah a gentle push.

57

Carole had just located a long black coat slung across the back of the couch. She held it up so that Deborah could slip her arms into it, while Max grabbed his own coat from a closet. "We'll be fine. Don't worry," she said.

"All right," Deborah said with a laugh. "I know you'll be fine. I just fed her a little while ago, but if she seems hungry later you can give her a bottle. There's one ready in the fridge. Just heat it up in the microwave and test it on your wrist to make sure it's not too hot. And by the way, clean diapers are in the closet upstairs."

"We know," Stevie said, rolling her eyes. "You told us all this stuff earlier, remember?" The girls had come by the house that morning to receive their instructions. Lisa had even written everything down in a notebook, mostly to make Deborah feel better.

Lisa looked up from her seat on the couch. "I just remembered one more question," she said, bouncing Maxi gently on her knees. "What time should we put her to bed? You didn't tell us that."

Max and Deborah both laughed. "You should try at around seven-thirty, I guess," Deborah said. "She didn't have much of a nap today, so you might get lucky."

"Got it," Stevie said. "Seven-thirty. Now get going, will you?"

Max and Deborah laughed again. Then, after a few more good-bye kisses for the baby and thanks for her baby-sitters, they were gone.

"Whew," Carole said, slumping down on the couch next to Lisa. "I thought they'd be here all night."

Stevie grinned. "I know." She grabbed one of Maxi's feet and tickled it. "Talk about parental jitters. Max asked us to look after the horses tonight, too, and he didn't give us one extra instruction about that." Since Max had given Red and the other stable hands the night off, the girls had volunteered to check on the horses once or twice during the evening.

"That's because he knows we know what we're doing with them," Lisa pointed out logically. "I don't blame him and Deborah for being more nervous about the baby. But they'll see. We'll have a great time tonight. Won't we, Maxi?" She gave the baby a hug, and Maxi squealed with delight, her eyes wide and trusting.

Carole stood up and took off her coat. She picked up Lisa's and held out her arm for Stevie's. "Want me to take that to the closet?" she offered.

"Thanks." Stevie slipped off Phil's jacket.

"Isn't that Phil's?" Lisa asked.

Stevie nodded and explained her reason for wearing it. "So I'll probably freeze again when we go down to check on the horses," she said complacently. "But it will be worth it." She checked her watch. "That reminds me. It's my turn to call next. Help me keep an eye on the time, okay?"

"Sure." Carole looked at her own watch. "It's only twenty of seven now. What do you want to do first?"

Lisa smiled. "That's easy," she said. "Let's play with the baby!"

The others were happy to comply. They crawled around on the carpet with Maxi and played with the toys that were scattered everywhere. Then Carole picked up the baby. "I have an idea," she said. "Let's play horsie."

She set Maxi astride her knee. Holding her hands so that the baby wouldn't fall, Carole bounced her leg up and down, pretending it was a horse.

Maxi giggled as she rode.

"Giddyup!" Carole cried.

After a few minutes, her leg got tired. She handed the baby to Lisa, who lay down on the couch on her back. Holding Maxi firmly by the tummy, Lisa raised her overhead, moving her back and forth. "Look," she said. "It's Maxi the jet plane. She's flying!"

"You call that flying? I'll show you flying." Stevie reached for the baby. She held her firmly by one leg, just below her diaper. With the other hand she supported the top half of Maxi's body. Then she walked around the room, making the baby swoop and dive through the air. "What's that in the sky?" she cried. "Is it a bird? Is it a plane? Is it a flying horse? No! It's Superbaby!"

Her friends laughed and clapped. "Save us, Superbaby," Carole called.

After a few more minutes of fun, Lisa checked her watch. "Hey, Stevie," she said. "It's time for your call."

"Oh!" Stevie handed Superbaby to Carole. "Thanks, Lisa," she said. "I'll be back in a minute."

She took the stairs two at a time and grabbed the phone in the upstairs hall. That would be more private than using the phone in the kitchen. Digging in her jeans pocket, she soon located the scrap of paper on which she had written down the direct phone number of Phil's hotel room. She dialed quickly and tapped her foot, waiting for someone to pick up.

Nobody did. Stevie tried again. Still no answer.

Phil had also given Stevie the number at the front desk. Stevie tried that next. The receptionist was very sympathetic, but she didn't get an answer when she tried the Marstens' room, either.

"Should I try again?" the receptionist asked.

Stevie sighed. "No, that's okay," she said. "Thanks anyway. I guess he's still at dinner." Phil had mentioned during the previous call that the family was getting ready to head for one of the resort's restaurants. He had thought he could be back in the room for Stevie's next call, but he must have gotten held up. Maybe they had had to wait for a table, or the service had been slow, or Phil had missed the monorail.

In any case, Stevie decided, she would just have to wait for eight o'clock to talk to him. It was no big deal. It was only an hour.

THE DOORBELL RANG at seven-thirty.

"Who could that be?" Lisa asked. She was struggling to fit one of Maxi's plump arms through the sleeves of her tiny nightgown. The baby was in a fresh diaper and almost ready for bed.

"There's only one way to find out," Stevie said, for once sounding almost as logical as Lisa. She walked out to the hall and peeked out one of the narrow windows that flanked the front door. Ms. Lynn was standing on the porch, looking very cold in a short wool coat and no hat.

"Brrr!" she exclaimed when Stevie opened the door and invited her in. "Thanks, Stevie. Isn't this supposed to be the American South? Back in Ohio we thought of

62

Virginia as practically tropical. Who would have known?"

Stevie laughed. "It's a little colder than usual this week," she admitted. "Did you see my note? Uh, I mean, Max's note?"

Ms. Lynn stuck her hand into her coat pocket and came up with a folded piece of paper. "Got it," she said. She paused and stared at Stevie. "By the way, what are you doing here? Are you Max's daughter or something? I didn't realize."

"Nothing like that," Stevie said. She led the way down the hall toward the living room. "In fact, if Max heard you he'd probably say something like 'God forbid.' " She grinned. "I'm just the baby-sitter for Max's real daughter, Maxi. You met her the other day."

As they entered the living room, Ms. Lynn looked around. "Well, hello," she greeted Carole and Lisa. "I see the whole gang's here. Are you the backup baby-sitters?"

"You could say that," Lisa replied, laughing. She held up Maxi, who finally had both arms in her nightgown sleeves. "Look, Maxi. It's your old pal, Ms. Lynn."

"Pleased to see you," the woman said to the baby with a grin, shaking her chubby fist playfully. Ms. Lynn smoothed down Maxi's hair, which was standing on end from Lisa's recent efforts to dress her. "I guess this means Max isn't here, right?"

Stevie confirmed that with a nod. "But he said you could just leave the check with us," she said. She grinned wickedly. "We promise not to spend it—at least not until after you leave."

Ms. Lynn laughed. "Funny," she said. She dug into her purse, located an envelope with Max's name on it, and handed it to Stevie, who propped it on the fireplace mantel where Max would be sure to see it. "But seriously, please let Max know how sorry I am that I was so late. My job can sometimes be unpredictable."

"Even on New Year's Eve?" Carole asked.

"Even on New Year's Eve," Ms. Lynn said. "I'm just glad Max wasn't waiting around for me. I was picturing him pacing up and down in the stable, staring at his watch, while his wife danced the night away at some fancy party."

The girls giggled. Ms. Lynn's description sounded awfully close to the truth. "He tried to wait for you," Lisa admitted with a grin. "Stevie wouldn't let him." The girls filled her in on The Saddle Club's holiday gift to Max and Deborah.

"What a fantastic idea," Ms. Lynn said when they were finished. She had taken Maxi from Lisa and was sitting on the couch, rocking the baby in her arms. Maxi was yawning, looking sleepy. "I remember when Britt was a baby. I didn't get much sleep, and I didn't have much time to do grown-up things. Babies are wonderful, but they can be draining if you don't get a break once in a while. I'm sure Max and Deborah appreciate this a lot."

"Speaking of Britt, we already have a few ideas about where to find a horse for her," Stevie said eagerly.

"That's great," Ms. Lynn said, sounding just as eager. "Tell me all about it." She moved Maxi's arm a little to get a look at her watch. "But you'd better make it the short version. I'm supposed to meet Britt at a party in a few minutes. She only knows a couple of people there, and I don't want her to be uncomfortable."

With a daughter as shy as Britt, Stevie supposed that Ms. Lynn had to think about that sort of thing a lot. She wondered what it would be like to be so shy that you couldn't have a good time at a party unless your mother was there. Then she decided she'd rather not know. It didn't sound like a very fun way to live.

"First of all," Stevie began, "almost all of Max's horses are for sale if the right buyer comes along. And he's got some great horses. Maybe Britt will hit it off with one of them." She shrugged. "But if not, don't despair. There are lots of other places to look." She glanced at the others, who nodded.

Carole then quickly described a few other local stables, including Cross County. "And there's one place that's even closer than those," she finished. "Hedgerow Farms."

"I think you mentioned that one before," Ms. Lynn said.

"It's a really great place," Carole said. "Even though they have had some bad luck lately."

Ms. Lynn looked interested. "What sort of bad luck?"

"First and worst of all, they had an outbreak of swamp fever a couple of months ago," Lisa said. Seeing Ms. Lynn's perplexed look, she explained. "That's a really bad disease for horses. The real name is equine infectious anemia. Hedgerow's breeding stallion died from it. And one of Pine Hollow's mares who was there to mate with him got it and died, too." She gulped and glanced at her friends. All three girls were remembering those terrible days, when Delilah, the beautiful palomino mare that had been a favorite Pine Hollow stable horse, had become sick after her return from Hedgerow.

Ms. Lynn didn't say anything for a moment. When Stevie looked at her, she saw that the woman had tears in her eyes. It made her like Ms. Lynn even more.

"Anyway," Carole said after a few more seconds of silence, "it could have been much worse, considering. Hedgerow only lost a few horses besides the stallion. And Delilah—the Pine Hollow mare—didn't pass it on to any other horses here."

"Still, it must have been terrible," Ms. Lynn said. "For all of you."

"It was," Carole said. "But that wasn't the end of Hedgerow's unlucky streak. Elaine, the manager, fell off the roof and broke her leg a week before Christmas."

"Oh no!" Ms. Lynn exclaimed. She shifted Maxi, who looked drowsier than ever, to her other arm and continued to rock her. "What on earth was she doing on the roof? Chasing a stray horse?"

Stevie giggled. "Not exactly," she said. "But that would make a good story, wouldn't it?"

Lisa rolled her eyes and smiled. "Actually, she was checking on a patch some workmen had made," she said. All three of the girls had heard the whole story from Max. Hedgerow's horses were housed in a large, old building that was starting to show its age. Not only was it old-fashioned, with unreliable wiring and dingy windows, but the structure itself was starting to get a little ramshackle. For that reason, Elaine had recently hired a construction company to build Hedgerow a new, more modern stable. Carole had seen the men laying the foundation the last time she had visited the farm with Judy, and she had told the others all about it. They couldn't wait to see it when it was finished.

"Max says Elaine is hobbling around in a cast these days, getting into as much trouble as ever," Stevie said with a grin.

Carole nodded. "And I know she has some young horses she and her staff have been training," she said. "Maybe one of them will be right for Britt."

"It sounds promising," Ms. Lynn said. She checked her watch. This time she had to move Maxi's foot to do it. "Oops, it's ten to eight already," she said. She stood up and gently handed the baby to Stevie. "I'd better go. But it's been great talking to you all."

"Same here," Lisa said. She glanced at Maxi worriedly. The baby was staring up at Stevie's face, blinking heavily. "I guess we lost track of the time. It's twenty minutes past Maxi's bedtime already."

Ms. Lynn chuckled as she buttoned her coat. "I wouldn't worry too much about that if I were you," she advised. She winked at the girls. "At that age, bedtimes are usually more of a hopeful guideline than a strict schedule."

Stevie looked down at Maxi. "Well, I don't think we have to worry about that," she said. "She looks pretty tired. We must have worn her out."

"I hope so . . . for your sake," the woman replied with a grin. Then she said good-bye and left, quickly closing the front door behind her to keep out the cold.

"I like her," Carole declared.

"Me too," Stevie said. "It's just too bad some of her personality didn't rub off on her daughter."

"Come on, Stevie. Be fair," Lisa said. "We hardly know Britt yet. I bet we'll love her once we all get used to each other." She headed toward the stairs. "Now, come on. Let's get this baby to bed."

All three girls went upstairs. They were on their way into the nursery when the phone rang.

Maxi jumped in Stevie's arms, startled at the sudden, loud sound. "Uh-oh," Stevie said. She was the closest to the phone, so she grabbed it, tucking it between her chin and her shoulder so that she could keep a good grip on the baby, who had started to wiggle. "Hello? Um, Regnery residence."

"Stevie?" came a familiar voice over the line.

"Deborah?" Stevie said. She gulped and looked down at Maxi, who was at this point definitely wide awake again. She quickly passed the baby to Carole, putting a shushing finger to her lips.

Fortunately, Maxi didn't make a peep. She just continued to pump her arms and legs and wiggle her body, forcing Carole to concentrate hard to keep her from squirming out of her grasp. Finally Carole gave up and sat down on the floor, forming a circle with her legs to keep Maxi corralled.

"Everything's fine here, Deborah," Stevie said into the phone. "We told you there was no reason to worry. Maxi? Oh, yes, she's in bed. She's sleeping like a . . . well, like a baby, I guess." She laughed.

"Really?" Deborah said. She sounded a little surprised.

Stevie smiled. She guessed that Deborah was impressed with The Saddle Club's baby-sitting skills. "Really," she fibbed, glancing at the baby, who was trying to make her escape by crawling over Carole's left knee. "We're all fine here. You should just forget about us and have a good time."

"Okay," Deborah said, still sounding uncertain. "Well, Max and I just ordered, and I thought I'd check in. Happy New Year." She said good-bye and hung up.

Stevie let out a sigh of relief as she hung up the receiver. "There," she said. "She never needs to know that we kept Maxi up past her bedtime. But we'd better get her settled." She glanced at her watch. "Phil is due to call in a few minutes."

The girls carried the baby into the nursery. Carole carefully lowered her into the crib and checked the sides to be sure they were locked in their upright position.

"Good night, little Maxi," Lisa said softly, leaning over to tickle the baby's plump belly. "Sleep tight. When you wake up, it will be a whole new year."

The other two girls said their good-nights as well. Maxi stuck her fingers in her mouth and watched them with wide eyes.

"She's so adorable," Carole whispered. "Come on. We'd better shut the door so that the phone won't startle her again when Phil calls. We can come up and check on her in a few minutes to make sure she got to sleep."

The others nodded and tiptoed out of the room. They left the door ajar just a couple of inches to let in some light from the hall.

"I'll turn down the ringer so that it won't bother her," Stevie whispered.

She quickly made the adjustment. Since the girls would be downstairs most of the time, she would be picking up Phil's next call on the kitchen phone, anyway. Then The Saddle Club headed for the stairs.

"Time for the rest of the party to start," Stevie whispered with a grin. "What should we do first? I vote for prank phone calls."

"Well, I guess we could—" Carole began.

She never got to finish the sentence. There was a loud, piercing scream from the direction of the nursery. It was Maxi, wailing at the top of her lungs, sounding as if her heart would break.

6

"I NEVER KNEW babies could have insomnia," Carole said twenty minutes later. She was in the living room, watching as Maxi crawled busily around the floor among her toys.

Lisa was sitting next to Carole on the couch. She sighed and rested her chin on her hand. "I never knew someone so cute could scream so loud," she said. "My head is still throbbing from the racket."

The girls had rushed back into the nursery at Maxi's first scream. As soon as they had entered the room, the baby had stopped crying. Within seconds, she was as happy as she had ever been.

72

But when the girls had once again tried to leave her alone in the crib, the same thing had happened. And again, as soon as they were back in the room, Maxi was happy again.

Lisa had rocked her for a few minutes. Then they had tried to leave again—with the same result.

This time, Stevie had suggested letting her cry for a little while. Her theory was that Maxi would wear herself out pretty soon and fall asleep.

It was only after ten straight minutes of ear-shattering screams that Stevie had remembered that her parents often tried the same trick with Stevie and her brothers when they were arguing or roughhousing or otherwise making noise. It never worked.

"I know what you mean, Lisa," Stevie groaned. She had collapsed on the floor next to the baby. Maxi giggled and crawled over her stomach. Stevie didn't move. "I feel like I've just been to the loudest rock concert in history. They say those can ruin your hearing." She grimaced. "If that's true, maybe Maxi won't be a horsewoman when she grows up after all. She'll be a rock star."

Lisa giggled. "She'd look awfully cute as the star of her own music video, wouldn't she?"

The others had to laugh at that. Carole leaned over and grabbed Maxi as she crawled toward the couch.

"Let's try rocking her," she said. "Maybe she'll get sleepy again like she did when Ms. Lynn was here."

While Carole was rocking Maxi, Lisa decided to heat up the baby's bottle. "If she has a little snack and sits with us for a while, she might calm down and fall asleep," she said.

Stevie nodded. "Good plan," she agreed. "Meanwhile, we can still get our own party started, right? Let's play a game of Monopoly or something. That should be easy to do while she's downstairs with us."

"Okay," Lisa said as she headed toward the kitchen for the bottle. "But make sure somebody holds on to her. We don't want her swallowing any of those little game pieces."

Stevie quickly located Max and Deborah's Monopoly game in a closet. She tossed a few of Maxi's toys into her playpen to create a clear space on the floor, then proceeded to set up the game board.

Carole looked over at the clock on the mantel. "So much for Maxi's seven-thirty bedtime," she said ruefully. "I hope she gets sleepy soon. It's already going on eight-thirty."

Stevie stopped straightening the play money and sat up quickly. "What did you say?" she asked. She didn't wait for Carole to answer. She jumped to her feet. "Eight-thirty! Oh, no. Phil missed our eight o'clock call!"

Lisa entered with the warm bottle just in time to hear her. "Are you sure about that?" she said. "Maybe you ought to check the answering machine. It was a little

74

noisy around here, you know. We might have missed the phone ringing."

Stevie gasped. "You're right! Especially since I turned down the ringer on the upstairs phone, remember?" She rushed into the kitchen and checked the answering machine beside the phone. Sure enough, the red message light was blinking.

Stevie played it back. Phil's familiar voice came out of the speaker, sounding tinny and far away.

"Uh, hi, Stevie," he said. "Sorry I missed you. And I'm sorry I missed your call at seven; I was late getting back from dinner, as you probably guessed. It's eight o'clock now. I'm going out for ice cream with my family. I'll make the next call, okay? My family's going out to see a fireworks display a little after nine, so it may be a few minutes early. I hope you're there. I'd really like to talk to you. Bye."

As the machine clicked off, Stevie let out a disappointed sigh. "I can't believe we missed each other again," she muttered. Still, there wasn't much she could do about it. They would just have to make up for it at nine o'clock. To be on the safe side, she picked up the phone's cordless receiver and checked the volume to make sure it was turned up nice and loud. She would take it into the living room with her. That way there was no way she could miss Phil's nine o'clock call.

She went back into the living room—and gasped at what she saw. Carole and Lisa were bent over their own arms, sprinkling little drops of milk from the bottle onto their inner wrists and looking perplexed. Meanwhile, Maxi was crawling across the Monopoly board, scattering paper money and plastic game pieces every which way. As Stevie watched, the baby picked up one of the game pieces and raised it toward her mouth.

"No!" Stevie shouted. She tossed the phone on an overstuffed chair near the stairs, jumped over a low side table, and scooped up the baby, prying the piece out of her tiny fist just in time.

Carole and Lisa looked up and quickly realized what was happening.

Lisa gasped. "Oh no!" she exclaimed. "I'm sorry, Stevie. I guess we got distracted. She didn't swallow anything, did she?"

"I don't think so," Stevie said. She had bent down to examine the remains of the game setup. "All the pieces seem to be here. Some of this money has a little baby drool on it, though."

Carole smiled with relief. "Thank goodness," she said.

And her friends knew that she wasn't talking about the drool.

Stevie looked down at the piece she was holding. She suddenly broke into a grin.

"What's so funny?" Lisa asked.

Stevie held out the piece. "Look which game piece Maxi decided to eat."

Carole and Lisa bent over her hand to see. Soon they

76

were grinning, too. "Of course," Carole said. "The horse and rider."

Maxi was cooing and reaching eagerly toward the milk bottle in Lisa's hand. Stevie handed Lisa the baby and started to clean up the Monopoly board.

"I guess the board games will have to wait until she falls asleep," she said.

Lisa nodded and settled down on the couch. Once the bottle was in her mouth, Maxi was silent except for an occasional slurp. "That's okay," Lisa said. "We can just talk for a while. Maybe get started on those resolutions."

"Okay," Carole said. "I have one. In the new year, I want to work really hard with Starlight on his half-halt. By this time next year, I want him to be able to do it perfectly every time I ask." The half-halt was a dressage move in which a horse hesitated, shifting its weight to its hindquarters and awaiting further instruction from its rider. Starlight was pretty good at it already, but Carole wanted him to be even better.

Stevie laughed. "It figures your first resolution has to do with horses," she teased. "Although actually, I was just thinking that one of my resolutions would be to practice braiding Belle's tail so that I can do it faster before shows."

"That's funny," Lisa said, looking up quickly. "That was one of mine, too."

"Really?" Stevie said. "You mean you're going to practice braiding Belle's tail, too? Great! Then I won't have to do it."

All three girls laughed at that. None of them was the least bit surprised that all of them had thought of horse-related resolutions.

"Speaking of braiding," Carole said, "which reminds me of tails, which reminds me of our tail hitching experiment the other day"—she paused for a breath before she went on—"have either of you thought up any more good ideas for the gymkhana? It will be here before we know it."

"Good point," Lisa said. The gymkhana was scheduled for the weekend before the girls' school vacations ended. "We've got to come up with some fun games."

"I wonder if Britt will want to ride in the gymkhana?" Carole said.

Stevie shrugged. "Of course she will," she said. "She may be shy, but that doesn't mean she's crazy. Who would want to miss it?"

"It would be great if we found her the perfect horse before then, wouldn't it?" Lisa mused. "I really hope we can help Ms. Lynn surprise her."

"Me too," Carole said. "I really think we should check out Hedgerow's horses first. When I was there with Judy a few weeks ago, I was very impressed with a couple of them. Maybe we can figure out a way to get Britt over there after New Year's without telling her why."

"Sort of a Welcome Wagon tour of the neighborhood?" Stevie offered.

Carole nodded and smiled. "Something like that."

Meanwhile Lisa was peering down at Maxi, who had stopped moving around in her arms. The baby's eyes were at half-mast. Lisa carefully plucked the almost empty bottle from her mouth. Maxi let it go without protest.

Noticing what Lisa was doing, Carole and Stevie kept quiet. Was the baby falling asleep at last?

Lisa stood up slowly and walked toward the stairs on tiptoes, gracefully avoiding the toys in her path. She had almost reached the stairs. Maxi hadn't moved. Her eyes were now all the way closed. Lisa held her breath.

Ring!

The shrill noise startled Lisa even more than it startled Maxi. And that was a lot. "The phone!" she cried as the loud ring came again. Maxi's eyes flew open, and she started to wail. "Get the phone!"

Carole looked toward the kitchen in confusion. But Stevie had suddenly remembered dropping the portable receiver on the chair. She also remembered that Phil had said he might call a few minutes early. It was twenty minutes to nine—maybe that was him now. She jumped to answer the phone.

"Hello?" she said breathlessly, speaking loudly enough to be heard over the crying baby.

Instead of Phil's voice, she heard Deborah's on the

other end of the line. "Stevie? It's me again," Deborah said.

"Oh," Stevie said, disappointed. "Um, I mean, hi. Where are you?"

"We're still at the restaurant," Deborah said. "We just ordered dessert and coffee. Is that Maxi crying in the background?"

"No, it's Lisa," Stevie joked weakly. "She lost at Monopoly." She decided there was no point in trying to hide the fact that Maxi was still awake. The baby was making that as clear as possible. Stevie stuck her finger in the ear that wasn't pressed against the phone. "Actually, Maxi doesn't seem very sleepy right now."

"She's all right, isn't she?" Deborah asked, sounding concerned. "We could head home right now if you think she might be sick—"

"No, no," Stevie said quickly. "She's fine. The phone just startled her, that's all." In fact, Maxi was quieting down already. Lisa had given her the stuffed horse to play with, and the baby let out a few more sobs and then stopped crying.

It took Stevie a few minutes to reassure Deborah that things were really all right. But finally Deborah seemed convinced. "Okay, then," she said. "Sorry about waking her up. Believe me, I know how she can be when she doesn't feel like sleeping. Anyway, the stage show here starts at around nine-thirty, so I probably won't have a chance to call again even if I'm tempted. We'll see you when we get home later."

"Okay," Stevie said. "Have a good time."

"Thanks," Deborah said. "You too. Oh, and tell Carole her father says hi. He's a couple of tables over from us."

Stevie hung up and passed the message on to Carole. "Deborah said she won't call anymore," she added.

Lisa had slung a towel over her shoulder and was burping Maxi, whose eyes were wide open once again. "Good," she said. "At this rate, we'll fall asleep before Maxi does."

Stevie glanced down at the phone, which she was still holding. "As long as she's awake anyway, maybe we should get started on those prank phone calls," she suggested. Phil probably wouldn't call for at least ten more minutes. Besides, the phone had call waiting. If it went off, Stevie could just hang up on Chad.

Carole sighed resignedly. "If you're going to do it, you might as well go ahead."

Stevie grinned. She was already dialing her home number.

After three rings, someone picked it up on the other end. "H'llo?" said an unfamiliar voice.

Stevie disguised her voice, making it as low and grown-up-like as possible. "Good evening," she said. "I'm trying to reach Mr. Chad Lake, please."

"Just a second." The phone clattered onto a hard surface.

A moment later, Chad's voice came over the line. "This is Chad Lake," he said uncertainly.

"Hello, Mr. Lake," Stevie said, still keeping her voice disguised. "This is Pat Patterson from radio station WQMZ in Washington. And this is a random call from our prize patrol."

Carole, who was listening, started to giggle. She clapped a hand over her mouth before Chad could hear her. Lisa just rolled her eyes and lowered Maxi to the floor next to her stuffed horse.

"Really?" Chad said, sounding suspicious but interested. "Is this really a radio DJ? Or is this a trick? . . . Stevie? Is that you?"

"This is no trick, young man," Stevie assured him in her disguised voice. "All you have to do to win a brand-new car is perform our challenge dare."

"What do I have to do?" Chad asked. By now he definitely sounded a lot more interested than suspicious. Stevie happened to know that he had already started bugging their parents about buying him his own car, even though he wouldn't even get his learner's permit for another two years.

"It's really very simple," Stevie told him. "Are you familiar with the song 'I'm a Little Teapot'?"

"Sure," Chad said.

By this time, Lisa was having a hard time controlling

her giggles, too. Stevie was careful to keep her fake voice steady. "All you have to do is sing that song to me as loudly as you can, right now. But you mustn't tell anyone in the house with you why you're doing it."

Chad hesitated. Stevie held her breath, waiting for an answer. Would his desire for that new car win out over his desire not to embarrass himself in front of all his friends? She certainly hoped so.

"You want that shiny new car, don't you, Mr. Lake?" she prompted.

"Well . . . ," Chad began after a second, "I only know one verse, but . . ."

At that moment, Maxi seemed to realize for the first time that her favorite toy was within her reach. She let out a loud crow of triumph and grabbed the stuffed horse from the floor. As she clutched it to her chest, she let out a few satisfied gurgles and one definite baby laugh.

"Hey," Chad said, suddenly sounding suspicious again—and more than a little annoyed. "Was that a baby in the background? I should have known it was you all along, Stevie!" He slammed down the phone.

Stevie groaned. "Maxi!" she chided, grabbing the baby and swinging her up into the air like Superbaby. "You ruined it! He was about to start singing. He would never have lived that one down."

"Too bad, Stevie," Lisa said with a laugh. "Now Chad will be on the lookout. You'll have a hard time fooling him again."

Carole nodded and grinned. "You might as well give up for tonight."

"Never," Stevie declared. She set Maxi down again and the baby raised her arms, squealing for more. "But I'm definitely going to have to wait until Superbaby goes to sleep."

"I CAN'T BELIEVE he hasn't called," Stevie muttered. She held her watch to her ear. "What time do you have, Lisa?"

Lisa sighed. "Twelve minutes after nine," she said. "One minute later than the last time you asked me."

"Why hasn't he called?" Stevie jumped out of the chair she was sitting in and started pacing back and forth across the living room. Her path was a twisting one, since she had to dodge the baby toys that still lay all over the floor.

Maxi watched Stevie with what seemed to be great interest. "Ga!" she cried happily, waving her stuffed horse in the air.

"That's what I say, too, Maxi," Carole said. "Ga." She rolled her eyes. Stevie hadn't taken her eyes off the clock—or the phone—since five minutes to nine. But Phil hadn't called.

"He's probably just running late again," Lisa said. "There's a lot to do at Disney World."

"I know," Stevie said. "But he said he was going to a fireworks display at nine. That means if he hasn't called by now, he's probably not going to call at all." She flopped back into the chair and crossed her arms over her chest.

Carole shifted her position on the couch and felt something jab her leg. She investigated and found a rattle sticking up between the cushions. "There's no sense just sitting there getting crankier and crankier," she told Stevie, pulling out the rattle and tossing it into the playpen. "Why don't you try calling him?"

Stevie looked over at her and frowned. Then she grinned. "You know, you sounded just like your dad for a second there." She stood up again and grabbed the phone from the mantel, where she had put it to keep it out of Maxi's reach.

She dialed Phil's room. There was no answer. Stevie let it ring seventeen times, then finally hung up in frustration. "He's not there," she said, her forehead beginning to crease into a frown again. "I guess he forgot all about me."

Lisa shot Carole a worried look. This wasn't good. They already had one baby who seemed as though she'd never sleep again. The last thing they needed was for Stevie to start pouting and acting like a *second* baby.

"I've got an idea," Carole announced suddenly. "I think we need to tire Maxi out or she'll stay awake all night. Why don't we take her down to the stable to say good night to the horses?"

Lisa sat up straight. "Great idea," she said. "That just might do the trick." *Besides,* she thought, *it also just might distract Stevie from brooding about Phil's missing their nine o'clock phone date. At least until* ten *o'clock rolls around.*

Stevie shrugged, but her frown faded a little. "I guess that could be fun," she said. "Maxi loves the stable. And we did promise Max we'd look in on the horses."

It was settled. Within minutes, the girls had Maxi bundled in so many layers of clothing that she was almost twice her actual size.

"That should do it," Lisa said, straightening the hat she had just tied under the baby's chin.

Carole giggled. "She looks like an overstuffed sausage," she said. She went to the closet and took out the girls' coats. She handed Lisa's to her, then looked doubtfully at Phil's jacket. "Are you sure this is going to be warm enough, Stevie?"

Stevie grabbed it. "I'll be okay," she said. "We don't have far to go."

Lisa found the infant carrier and slipped it on before putting on her coat. "I'll carry Maxi down in this," she said. "She can ride under my coat and stay warm."

The air outside had grown even colder, and the wind was blowing harder than ever. Carole had to grab at her knit cap to keep it from flying away.

"Are you sure this is a good idea?" Lisa shouted over the sound of the wind. She zipped her jacket a little higher, covering Maxi up to just below her eyes.

"Just come on!" Carole shouted back. She headed down the hill toward the stable building, her body bent forward against the wind. The others huddled deeper into their coats and followed.

Soon they were letting themselves into the cozy warmth of the stable building.

"Whew!" Stevie exclaimed. She whipped her hat off and gave one last shudder as her body welcomed the heat. "That's what I call cold."

Lisa unzipped her jacket and checked on Maxi. The baby seemed fine. Even the tip of her nose was only a little bit pink from the cold. "It wouldn't be so bad if it weren't for that wind," she said. "Now I know what people mean when they talk about a howling gale." She could still hear the wind rattling the eaves and hurling itself against the outside of the building. But inside, the more immediate sounds were those of the horses, shifting and nickering sleepily in their stalls or munching on a bedtime snack of hay.

"We'd better unwrap Maxi a little bit," Carole pointed out. "It's pretty warm in here, and we don't want her to get overheated."

They removed the baby's hat and a few layers of her clothing. "Okay, that's better," Stevie said. She hoisted Maxi onto one hip. "Now let's go say hello to some of our four-footed friends. Okay, Maxi?"

She started down the nearest row of stalls. Most of the inhabitants had stuck their heads out over their half doors when the girls had entered. And most of them were eager to snuffle at the baby as Stevie held her up to pat their big, soft muzzles.

"See?" Stevie said as Maxi gurgled at Nickel, a sweet gray stable pony. "It's just as we suspected. This is her natural environment."

Carole was happy to see that her friend seemed to have stopped brooding about her missing boyfriend. "I'm not arguing with you on that one," she said with a laugh. "Although I feel I should point out that Maxi seems pretty happy just about anywhere except for her bed."

Coconut, the flaxen chestnut gelding, was in the stall next to Nickel's. Once again, Stevie held the baby up to pat the horse. Coconut pricked his ears forward curiously, then lowered his head toward the tiny visitor. Maxi stretched out her hand to touch the horse on the nose and let out a delighted chortle. The horse gazed at her with his big, liquid brown eyes.

"If I didn't know better, I'd swear Coconut was smiling," Lisa commented softly. "He must like babies."

Carole watched as the horse started snuffling at Maxi's downy brown hair. The baby giggled and threw up her hands. "I guess he does," Carole said with a smile. "Although I think Coconut pretty much likes everyone."

They moved on down the stable row. Maxi cooed and chuckled at the other stable horses and boarders, from the Arabian gelding Barq to the Thoroughbred mare Calypso to Polly Giacomin's horse, Romeo.

The girls skirted the stall where Geronimo, Pine Hollow's resident stallion, lived. They knew that stallions were more unpredictable than geldings or mares, so they didn't take the baby to meet him. As they rounded the corner, they found themselves standing before the stall of an even-tempered Appaloosa gelding named Chip, short for Chippewa.

Chip seemed as curious about the baby as most of the other horses had been. Stevie's arms were getting tired, so she handed Maxi to Carole and stretched. She was also getting warm, so she removed her jacket and hung it over the door of an unoccupied stall across the aisle.

"Say hi to Chip, Maxi," Carole said encouragingly.

"Ga!" Maxi exclaimed, stretching out both arms toward the horse.

Carole glanced at the others and shrugged. "I'd say that's close enough, wouldn't you?" she said.

Lisa and Stevie leaned against the door of the empty

stall and watched as the baby tugged on Chip's mane. "He's really a patient horse, isn't he?" Lisa mused.

Stevie nodded. "I've only ridden him once or twice, but he's a doll," she said. "He's superfriendly and never fights his rider."

"Are you thinking what I'm thinking?" Lisa asked.

"Only if you're thinking that Chip could be a candidate for Britt," Stevie replied with a grin, knowing very well that Lisa was thinking exactly that.

Carole twisted her head around. Maxi was busily rubbing Chip's neck with her little hands. "Look, she's grooming him," she said. "What are you guys talking about?"

Lisa told her. "I was just thinking about all the horses here," she said. "Even though it would be weird in one way if Max sold one of his school horses to the Lynns, it wouldn't be in another way, since Britt would be sure to board him right here. And there are lots of really great horses at Pine Hollow to choose from."

Carole nodded thoughtfully. She walked down to the next stall, where a chestnut gelding named Comanche lived. The horse snorted suspiciously at the baby, but he soon gave in to his curiosity and lowered his head to be patted. "There *are* a lot of great horses here," Carole said. "But I don't think all of them are that great for someone like Britt. She's so shy and timid, but she's also a really good rider. That's kind of a weird combination, don't you think?"

"I see what you mean," Stevie said. "She needs a nice, friendly horse that won't scare her, like Chip. But she also needs a confident, talented horse that will challenge her skills, like Comanche."

Lisa gazed at Comanche, then turned to look at Chip, who still had his head out and was watching them. "In that case, maybe neither one is the right horse for her." She sounded a little disappointed.

"Don't worry," Carole said. "Even if they're not right, another horse might be. Barq, for instance, or Diablo. Or maybe a horse from another stable." She shrugged. "When it comes right down to it, Britt is the only one who can really decide. All we can do is try to narrow down her choices for her so she'll have an easier time picking her new horse."

"And try to keep her from realizing that's what she's doing," Stevie put in.

They were still talking about Britt a few minutes later when they reached Belle's and Starlight's stalls, which were next to each other. Lisa held the baby while Stevie and Carole greeted their horses and wished them a happy New Year. Carole found a few carrot sticks in her coat pocket, and she gave Stevie and Lisa some for their horses.

As she let herself out of Belle's stall, Stevie glanced at her watch. "Uh-oh," she said. "It's almost ten minutes to ten already. We'd better get back to the house. I don't want to miss another call."

Carole noticed that although Stevie seemed concerned, she no longer seemed annoyed or angry. *That's the great thing about horses,* Carole told herself happily. *They can always make you feel better—about anything!*

The girls walked back to the entrance, where they had left Maxi's outer clothing. Carole started to bundle up the baby while her friends watched.

As Carole slipped a tiny wool sweater over Maxi's head, the baby's mouth stretched open in a big yawn. "Aha!" Carole exclaimed. "It looks like our plan might have worked. She's getting sleepy."

"Don't count on it," Stevie advised. "My guess is that she knows she's about to leave the stable and she's bored already."

Lisa grinned. "She really does seem to love the horses, doesn't she?" she said. It wasn't the first time she had noticed it, but the fact never ceased to delight her. "It's almost as if she knows her destiny as Max the Fourth." Maxi's father's full name was Maximilian Regnery III. Even though Maxi's name was Maxine and didn't have a number after it, The Saddle Club still thought of her as Max IV, born and bred to carry Pine Hollow into the next generation.

"I think you're right," Carole said. "It's fate." She grinned. "No matter what Deborah thinks about that!"

The others laughed. Then Carole finished tying Maxi's hat on and tucked her back into the carrier, which Stevie had volunteered to wear this time.

"I'm hoping Maxi will help keep me warm on the way back up," she admitted as the baby nestled against her and let out another yawn.

The girls braced themselves as Lisa swung open the door. The wind was still blowing furiously in harsh, whipping gusts that made the surrounding treetops swing crazily against the moonlit sky.

"What a night!" Carole called.

The others didn't answer. They raced around the building and across the lawn, cutting through the small pasture at one corner of the stable. Stevie watched the ground carefully as she ran. She didn't want to trip while she was carrying the baby. But she also wanted to get back inside as fast as she possibly could. It was freezing out there!

Soon the girls were jogging up the slight incline that indicated where the stable grounds ended and the Regnery yard began. "Am I going crazy, or is the wind starting to die down a little?" Lisa said.

Carole started to nod. It did seem a little calmer than it had only a couple of minutes before when they had emerged. But before she could say so, she was almost bowled over by another gust, stronger than ever. It whipped around the house in front of them and then swirled around them, driving small branches, dead leaves, and other bits of debris against them. Carole had to grab on to a nearby tree trunk to avoid being knocked off her feet by its wild strength.

Stevie quickly shielded the baby's face from the worst of it, crouching low to keep her balance. "Wow!" she said a second later when the gust had disappeared as quickly as it had come. "What was that?"

Lisa brushed a soggy oak leaf off her shoulder and shook her head. "I don't know," she said. "But whatever it was, it seems to have been the grand finale."

The girls paused and listened. Sure enough, the wind was barely audible now. The wild gust seemed to have chased away the last bit of the storm. Even the air felt a little warmer.

The girls continued up the hill at a walk. "What weird weather," Stevie said. She looked down at Maxi. The baby didn't even seem to have noticed the big gust of wind. She was blinking sleepily beneath her warm cap.

"Tell me about it," Carole agreed. "I bet that last gust brought a few trees down. We're lucky the power didn't go out."

Lisa glanced ahead at the house. Lights shone brightly from several windows. "Good point," she said. "I'd hate to have to baby-sit in the dark."

"I don't know about that," Stevie pointed out with a twinkle in her eye. "Maybe total darkness would be the one thing that would put Maxi to sleep."

Carole laughed. "If she doesn't stay down this time, maybe we'll have to try that," she said. "It would be worth sitting in the dark for a few minutes to avoid another big crying spell."

"I hate to point this out," Lisa said, "but there's at least one light we can't turn out." She pointed above their heads at the almost full moon, which was casting a silvery glow over the entire area.

The girls fell silent as they covered the last few yards to the house. The sound of the ringing phone came to them clearly as they climbed the steps to the porch.

Stevie gasped. "Phil!" she exclaimed. "I've got to get it before the machine picks up again!" She unlatched the front door quickly and rushed inside, baby and all.

Carole and Lisa followed more slowly. "I sure hope that's Phil," Carole said. "If it's just Deborah calling to check in at intermission, there could be trouble."

Meanwhile, Stevie had grabbed the phone just as the answering machine clicked on.

"Hello, this is Deborah," the recorded tape began. "Max and I can't come to the phone right now, but . . ."

"Hold on!" Stevie shouted into the phone. "I'm here, I've got it. Let me just—" She hurried into the kitchen and jabbed at the Off button on the answering machine. "There," she said with satisfaction when the tape cut off. "Sorry about that. Phil? Is that you?"

But it wasn't Phil's voice that answered her. It wasn't Deborah's, either. It was a woman's voice that Stevie didn't recognize at first. The caller sounded terribly distraught, and for a moment Stevie couldn't even figure out what she was saying.

"I'm sorry," she said. "Are you sure you have the right number? This is the Regnery residence."

The caller took a deep, audible breath and spoke again, more slowly this time. "No, no, please don't hang up," she said shakily. "This is Elaine, from Hedgerow Farms, and I'm calling for Max. I need his help. My stable roof just collapsed!"

STEVIE TOOK A deep breath and tried to keep her voice steady. "Did you say your stable roof collapsed?" she asked the woman on the phone. Visions of terribly injured horses flashed through her mind.

Carole and Lisa gasped behind her, but Stevie concentrated on what Elaine was saying. "That's right," the woman said. "The wind did it. Our stable is old, and—by the way, who is this? Deborah?"

"No," Stevie said. "It's Stevie Lake. Lisa, Carole, and I are baby-sitting."

"Oh, yes, of course. I remember you, Stevie. Lisa, too. And of course I know Carole." Elaine paused and gulped.

98

"But I must admit I would be happier to be talking to Max right now. I was hoping he could help me get my horses out. And maybe keep them overnight for me. It's too cold for them to stay out in the pasture, and—"

"Wait a minute," Stevie interrupted. "You need help getting the horses out? Does that mean they're okay?" She glanced around at her friends, who were listening intently to her side of the conversation. Carole was biting her fingernails. Lisa had lifted Maxi out of the carrier and was hugging the baby so tightly that Maxi was squirming in protest.

"I'm not sure," Elaine said, sounding desperate. "I think they are—at least most of them. Only part of the roof actually caved in, and most of it was over the tack room and bathrooms, thank heavens. But I'm afraid the structure still isn't safe, and I want to get them out as quickly as possible. I'm alone here tonight because of the holiday, and I'm not exactly mobile. My leg is in a cast."

"Oh, right," Stevie said. "Max mentioned that." One part of her mind was racing. She could imagine how terrified the Hedgerow horses must be after part of their home had collapsed around them. Even if they hadn't been injured in the accident, they could panic and hurt themselves in the aftermath. It was terrible. Why did such awful things keep happening to that unfortunate stable? It just didn't seem fair.

But another part of Stevie's mind stayed surprisingly

calm. That part knew that there was only one thing to do. And that part retained control.

"Don't worry, Elaine," Stevie said. "We'll be right there."

Ten minutes later, The Saddle Club was back at the stable. Lisa was wearing the infant carrier with Maxi in it, and she stood back and watched as her friends hurried to tack up Starlight and Belle.

"I'm still not sure this is a good idea," she said worriedly as Stevie rushed by with Belle's bridle slung over one arm and her saddle balanced over the other. Carole was right behind her with Starlight's tack. "We could try calling Max at the restaurant. I bet he and Deborah would get back here as quickly as they could."

Stevie shook her head. "It wouldn't be quick enough," she said. She tossed Belle's saddle over the door of her stall and led the mare out into the aisle. The horse seemed surprised at the late-night outing, but she stood calmly while Stevie bridled her and then tossed her lead line to Lisa to hold while she hoisted the blanket, saddle pad, and saddle onto Belle's back. "It would take them at least forty-five minutes, even without the holiday traffic and bad weather. Besides, we might not be able to reach them right away if they're in the middle of the show."

"But it may not be safe . . . ," Lisa began helplessly. She glanced down at Maxi. With all the excitement, the baby was wide awake once again. She stared around with wondering eyes as Carole bustled past, carrying a fistful of lead lines.

"I'll bring these along. Elaine said her tack room is in bad shape, right?" Carole asked Stevie.

Stevie nodded as she cinched Belle's girth. "It sounds like most of it got crushed under the fallen roof," she said. "I can carry some of those if you want." She tucked a few of the lead lines into the pocket of Max's warmest coat, which she had borrowed from the front closet. It was a little big on her, but she was sure she could still ride in it. And she definitely needed something warm for this job.

"You don't mind staying with the baby, do you, Lisa?" Carole asked, glancing over her shoulder at her friend.

Lisa shrugged. "I don't know," she said. "I mean, someone has to. And your horses are much more reliable than Prancer would be for something like this. So it's the logical choice. But I'm still not sure you're going to be able to get all those horses back through the woods by yourselves. Elaine can't ride with her broken leg, so it will just be the two of you."

Hedgerow lay less than two miles from Pine Hollow as the crow flew. By the winding country roads of the area, however, it was much farther. In fact, the only thing lying between the two stables was the thickly wooded parkland that began just behind Max's house. Stevie and Carole had decided that they could herd Elaine's horses along the main trail through those woods. The path had

101

two advantages. It was a popular hiking spot, so it was worn smooth enough to offer little danger of injury to the horses' delicate legs and feet. And for most of its length it was flanked by enough trees and underbrush to discourage even the most skittish horse from running off from the group.

As soon as she had hung up the phone with Elaine, Stevie had pointed out that the wooded trail was the best—perhaps the only—option open to them. The Hedgerow horses couldn't stay in their old stable that night, for obvious reasons. Their new stable wasn't anywhere near finished. And the weather was too severe for them to stay outdoors, even for one night. That left Pine Hollow, which had enough empty stalls to house most of the horses. The rest could stay in the indoor ring.

The trouble was getting them there. Elaine couldn't drive a horse van with her broken leg, and the girls were too young to drive. And even if they could locate an adult with a license on this holiday evening, they would only be able to transport a few horses at a time. It would be better to get them all inside as soon as possible, especially since they were bound to be worked up and sweaty from fear and excitement after the collapse of the roof. The trail was their best hope.

Carole paused and thought about what Lisa had just said. Even after the swamp fever disaster, Hedgerow had almost two dozen horses living in the stable. How would she and Stevie be able to herd them all back to Pine Hollow? Especially if any of them were injured . . .

"It really would be safer with three people," Carole agreed slowly. "That way one of us could lead the way, another could bring up the rear, and the third could stay in the middle to reassure the horses and keep an eye on them in case any tried to get away."

Stevie shrugged. "We'll just have to make do," she said. "Even if it means making two or three separate trips. We can't leave Maxi here by herself. Maybe Lisa can try my house again in a few minutes." The girls had tried to reach Stevie's parents, hoping they could step in as baby-sitters. But the line had been busy, and Stevie had guessed that Chad and his friends were making some prank phone calls of their own.

"Anyway, I guess Prancer really would be pretty useless out there," Lisa admitted. Thanks to Lisa's hard work with her, the mare had become much better about staying calm and obeying her rider. But in an emergency situation, Lisa wasn't sure she could control her adequately. The mare was still too green.

Carole shrugged. "I wish that were our only problem," she said. "If it were, you could just ride a different horse." She nodded toward the baby. "That's the real problem. We have a responsibility here and nobody to help us out."

"It's too bad Maxi's not a few years older," Stevie said

with a weak grin. "Otherwise she'd be able to ride along and help us out. In fact, she'd probably be leading the way in typical Regnery style."

Carole grimaced. "Oh, right," she said sarcastically. "I'm sure Deborah would love that . . ."

Her voice trailed off. She was staring at Maxi. Or, more specifically, at the carrier that Maxi was snuggled into. *What if . . . ?*

"I have an idea," she said. "It may be a little crazy, but it just might work."

"HOW ARE YOU doing back there, Lisa?" Stevie asked, twisting around on Belle's back to talk to her friend, who was riding behind her.

"So far, so good," Lisa said. "You were right about Topside. He's really alert!"

"Good," Carole called from behind Lisa. "I was a little worried, since you've never really ridden him before. But his training could come in handy on the way back."

The three girls were trotting briskly down the wooded trail on their way to Hedgerow Farms. Lisa was riding Topside, one of Max's school horses. Like Prancer, Topside was a Thoroughbred. Unlike Prancer, however, he had been trained for the show ring, not the racetrack. In fact, he had once belonged to one of the top competitive riders in the country. Stevie had ridden Topside regularly before buying Belle, and although the tall bay gelding definitely had a mind of his own, he was also one of the most responsive and intelligent horses she had ever known. That was why she and Carole had chosen him for Lisa tonight. They would need smart and obedient horses to keep the frightened Hedgerow herd in line. Lisa had been a little nervous about riding the spirited gelding. But after a few minutes on his back, she had started to relax, delighted with his responsiveness. He wasn't the easiest horse she had ever ridden, but her riding had improved a lot lately. She could handle him.

Carole signaled for Starlight to lengthen his stride a bit more as the others pulled farther in front of her. Then she looked down. Maxi looked back up at her, her eyes wider and brighter than ever.

"Hey, you guys," Carole called to her friends. "I think Maxi likes riding!" As soon as Carole had mentioned her idea to bring Maxi with them in the infant carrier, Lisa had remembered something. Deborah had told her that Max kept threatening to take the baby for a ride in the carrier, and that had been all the encouragement The Saddle Club had needed. They would bring the baby with them!

Since Carole was the best rider of the three, she had volunteered to be the one to carry Maxi. And so far, the experiment had gone very well. She had been worried about jostling Maxi while mounting, so Stevie had held the carrier until Carole was safely in the saddle. Then it had been a simple matter to take the carrier and fasten it on while Lisa held Starlight's head to keep him still.

Of course, that hadn't stopped all three girls from pausing for longer than usual at the lucky horseshoe. The battered shoe nailed to the wall by the door was Pine Hollow's lucky charm. No one who had touched it before setting off on a ride had ever been seriously hurt. The girls hoped its luck would help them tonight. Carole even stretched Maxi's little arm to brush the horseshoe with the baby's fingertips.

"You're never too young for good luck," she had told Maxi.

Now she glanced down at the baby again. Despite all The Saddle Club's jokes, Carole had been afraid that Maxi wouldn't like riding. Starlight's gaits felt very smooth and easy to Carole, but she knew that a tiny baby might have a different opinion.

Maxi, however, didn't seem to mind the jostling and bouncing one bit. If anything, she appeared to be enjoying herself.

"I guess that Superbaby thing was no fluke," Carole called ahead to Stevie, remembering the swooping and swaying game Stevie had invented earlier. "Maxi likes action and excitement."

"Of course she does," Stevie called back, sounding a bit smug. "I could have told you that. She's a natural horsewoman, after all."

Carole laughed. She took both of Starlight's reins in one hand so that she could tug the baby's hat a little lower over her forehead and ears. Fortunately, the wind really had died down for the moment, and the air, while still cold, was no longer as biting as it had been earlier that evening. Still, the girls hadn't taken any chances. Maxi was bundled up as tight as ever.

"Snug as a bug in a rug," Carole murmured, remembering the phrase her father sometimes used when he tucked her in at night.

The three girls covered the miles to Hedgerow as quickly as possible. Finally the woods started to thin out and lights twinkled at them through the trees.

"There's Hedgerow," Stevie said, urging Belle into a canter. "Let's go."

The others followed. Carole checked on Maxi, who was fine. Then she glanced forward to check on Lisa. She looked as comfortable on Topside as if she'd been riding him for years. Carole looked farther ahead at the buildings that were just becoming visible as the three horses left the tree line behind and cantered side by side across a small pasture.

What she saw made her gasp in horror. She had seen the big, old-fashioned stable at Hedgerow many times. But she had never seen it looking like this.

The main length of the building stretched across the flat ground just ahead of them. The left side of the stable looked much the same as always. But the right side, which, as Carole knew from previous visits, held the main stable entrance as well as the tack room, a small indoor exercise ring, and a few big box stalls, looked as though a giant had wandered by and stomped on it. A large section of the roof had ripped free and caved into the stable in huge, jagged chunks. Several pieces stuck up at odd angles, while others had disappeared entirely into the building's interior.

"I hope there were no horses in the stalls on that end," Carole said, staring at the destruction.

The others just nodded grimly and kept riding.

When they got closer, Carole spotted Elaine. The woman was hobbling awkwardly out of the smaller back entrance on the far left side of the stable. She had one crutch tucked under her arm, and her other hand was clutching a lead line. A small bay horse was on the other end of the line, dancing nervously and rolling its eyes until the whites showed.

"Hold this," Stevie said. In one smooth motion, she leaped out of Belle's saddle and tossed the reins to Lisa, who caught them expertly.

Stevie rushed forward to help Elaine. Soon she had taken the bay horse's lead and was coaxing it toward a small paddock that lay between the back entrance of the stable building and the long, low-slung house where

Elaine lived. Carole could see that there were already more than half a dozen horses milling around in the paddock.

"It looks like you've been busy," Carole called as Elaine approached The Saddle Club's horses, leaning heavily on her single crutch. When Elaine got closer, Carole noticed that the woman's forehead was beaded with sweat.

"Thank goodness you're here," Elaine gasped. "I've been doing the best I can to get them out, but I feel like I'm going to collapse. I've called the police for help, but they're not sure when they can get here. I guess this is a busy night for them."

Carole was already unhooking the straps of Maxi's carrier. "Go inside and rest," she ordered Elaine. "And take this baby with you. She shouldn't stay out here in the cold."

Elaine looked startled, but she reached out to take Maxi as Carole carefully handed down the carrier. "Who is this?" she asked.

"It's Max's daughter, Maxi," Stevie said as she rejoined them. "I told you we were baby-sitting, remember?"

Elaine smiled for a split second as she glanced down at Maxi, who stared back up at her curiously. Then the woman looked over at what remained of her stable, and her face grew grim once again.

"I've got to get off this leg for a few minutes," she said. "But I'll be back out to help as soon as I can. I'll rig up something inside that will make do as a playpen. Okay?"

Carole nodded. She couldn't imagine that Elaine would recover anytime soon. But she didn't say so. "Sounds good," she said.

"I've been bringing out the horses closest to the door first," Elaine told them as she hooked the straps of the infant carrier around her shoulders and then grasped her crutch tightly again. "There's a lot of debris farther in, and with this leg I haven't been able to get back there. So I don't know if . . ." Her voice trailed off, and her face twisted with pain. This time, the girls were pretty sure her broken leg had nothing to do with it. She was afraid for her horses, afraid that some of them might have been injured in the accident—or worse.

"We'll do everything we can," Lisa assured her quickly. They couldn't promise any more than that.

"Okay," Elaine said. "But keep your riding hard hats on, just in case. And be careful. If the wind starts up again, come right out. I don't want you to take any chances."

The girls were already busy tying their horses' lead lines to a nearby fence post. Then Carole handed Lisa a few of the extra lead lines she had brought, and the girls raced toward the stable.

Miraculously, the electric lights hadn't gone out in the collapse. As they entered through the back door, they saw that the stable aisle was brightly lit.

It was also noisy. Terrified whinnies and neighs came from every side. Several horses had their heads stuck out over their half doors as far as they could reach. Carole could only assume that the others were huddled in the backs of their stalls. At the far end of the aisle, she saw where the collapse had taken place. Dust was still floating, obscuring her view, but she could see the jagged edge of a large piece of roof. She shuddered, thinking how close it had come to the farthest stall in the row.

"Uh-oh," Stevie said, pointing to a stall about halfway down the aisle.

The others looked and immediately recognized the problem. A large gray horse had managed to get one of its forelegs hooked over the top of the half door.

Carole was already running down the aisle. "He must have been rearing in the stall," she shouted. "Quick— we've got to calm him down before he breaks that leg."

The horse was terrified. He neighed repeatedly as the girls approached.

Carole forced herself to slow down as she neared the stall. She began talking soothingly to the animal, hardly noticing what she was saying.

The horse pricked his ears toward her, seeming to listen. He stopped thrashing about almost immediately.

"It's okay, boy," Stevie said, adding her own soothing voice to Carole's. "We're here to help."

"I know this horse," Carole said quietly, keeping her voice as soft and gentle as before. "Judy had to give him some shots last summer, and I helped. We may be okay. He's actually very calm, and he loves people."

Her words were soon proved correct. As soon as the girls touched him, the gray horse seemed to understand that they were there to help. Unhooking his leg was tricky, but the horse was cooperative, and the girls managed it.

"I'll take him out," Lisa said. There was a halter hanging beside the stall door. Lisa slipped it on the gray and hooked a lead line to it. The horse followed her without protest.

"That's one down," Stevie said. "Let's hope the others are all that appreciative."

They weren't. Some of the panicky horses did their best to kick or bite the girls who were trying to rescue them. Others backed into the farthest corners of their stalls and tried to elude them. But most seemed eager to escape from their suddenly terrifying stable and followed gladly as the girls led them, one by one, to the small paddock outside.

As she released a relatively calm Appaloosa mare into the now crowded paddock, Carole paused to scan the growing herd. So far they had been lucky. A few of the horses had cuts or bruises from throwing themselves around in their stalls. But none of the horses the girls had released so far seemed to have sustained any more serious injuries.

"Let's hope it stays that way," Carole muttered, crossing her fingers as she ran back to the stable to rejoin her friends.

She found that Stevie had just hooked a lead line to a plump gray pony. Despite his rather sleepy appearance, the little horse let out a quick buck and kick as Stevie tugged on the line.

"I'm glad Elaine hasn't replaced her stallion yet," Stevie said, taking a firmer grip on the line. "Otherwise we might have some real problems."

Carole hadn't even thought of that. Hedgerow's stallion had been the first casualty of the swamp fever outbreak. And while Elaine had started searching for a replacement, she hadn't found a stallion she liked yet. It was a good thing, too. Trying to deal with an unpredictable stallion in a frightening situation like this would have been downright dangerous for the girls. Carole wondered at the fact that something that seemed like pure, horrible bad luck—like swamp fever—could actually have a little bit of good luck hidden within it.

But there was no time for philosophizing. There were still four or five horses left to rescue. Carole hurried to the next stall, where a slender chestnut mare was letting out shrill screams of terror and dismay.

It took Carole a few minutes to coax the frantic mare out of her stall. By the time she released her into the paddock, Stevie and Lisa had freed the last few horses in the stable row.

"Is that it?" Carole asked Stevie, who was patting a bay

gelding on the rump to urge him into the ring with his stablemates.

Stevie's face was grim. "Bad news," she said. "We've got all the horses out of the main row, but there's still a horse trapped inside. It must be in one of those box stalls you were talking about. The ones at the other end."

Carole gasped. "You mean there's a horse trapped under the roof?"

"I can't tell where he is," Lisa said, "but he's definitely alive. As Stevie and I were bringing these last two out, we could hear him whinnying. We didn't realize before that it was coming from back there because the other horses were making so much noise."

Carole was already heading back toward the building. "We've got to find him." She ran into the stable and down the aisle past the now empty row of stalls. At the end, she skidded to a stop. She heard what her friends had been talking about: A horse's terrified screams were echoing through the damaged building from somewhere in the direction of the crash.

Stevie and Lisa were right behind her. "You know this stable better than we do," Lisa told Carole. "Lead the way."

"I'll try," Carole said, staring at the jumble of debris that blocked their path. She waved a hand to try to clear the dust, patted her hard hat to make sure it was settled firmly on her head, and plunged into the destruction.

She scrabbled over a roof section that had broken into

a dozen ragged pieces when it had landed on the bathroom fixtures below. Her friends followed. The area where the large box stalls had been was just beyond the bathrooms, if Carole remembered correctly. It was a little hard to tell. Everything looked a lot different now under all the rubble.

The lights were out in this section. Fortunately, the moon was still up, and its white glow gave enough light for Carole to see her way. Off to the left, there was the sound of gushing water—probably from a broken pipe, Carole thought distractedly. She was listening to the horse, which was still crying out from somewhere ahead. All they had to do was follow the sound.

"We're coming, boy!" Carole called out.

"Or girl," Stevie added.

The horse fell silent for a moment, and the girls paused, holding their breath. Then the animal let out another squeal of fear.

"That way," Stevie said, crawling up next to Carole and pointing to the right.

Carole nodded and adjusted her direction.

The neighs got louder. The girls reached an area where a large, intact section of the roof had tipped into the building at a sharp angle. Stevie gave it a kick. When it didn't move, they crawled beneath it, then emerged into what Carole guessed had once been the indoor exercise ring. Just beyond the ring was the area where the box stalls had been.

116

The ring's floor was mostly clear, and the girls ran across it toward the sound of the terrified horse, which they still couldn't see.

Carole was in the lead. She rounded the corner formed by a jagged piece of wall that had been broken off above their heads, then skidded to a stop. The door of the stall had been knocked down by a chunk of falling plaster, so Carole could see the horse inside.

It was a big chestnut gelding—at least Carole guessed he was a chestnut. The horse was so covered with dust that it was hard to tell. He was lying on his side in the stall, twisting his neck around to let out his sharp, terrified calls. And Carole immediately saw why the horse was so frightened.

He was trapped under a section of the roof!

STEVIE AND LISA arrived a second later and took in the situation.

"Oh, my gosh," Lisa breathed in horror.

The horse couldn't quite see them from his position, but he could tell they were there. His cries grew louder and more insistent, and his eyes rolled wildly as he tossed his head. The girls could hear at least a couple of his hooves pounding on the underside of the wooden planking that was pinning his body to the ground.

Stevie was already examining the large piece of debris. "This is just plywood or something," she reported to the others. "I don't think it's the actual roof. It looks like it broke off the hayloft."

Carole had pushed her way past a fallen beam to enter the stall. She approached the horse's head cautiously, murmuring soothing words to him. But she was afraid to get close enough to touch him. The horse was so agitated that she thought he might bite out of pure terror.

"Come on," Stevie called. "Help me out here. I think we can move it."

Carole backed out of the stall and went to help. Lisa, too, joined Stevie along the edge of the fallen wood.

Now they could all see what must have happened. When the roof had collapsed in that section of the stable, it had brought down part of the hayloft with it. Somehow, a large chunk of the loft floor had ended up on top of the pile of debris, while the actual roof had flown off in another direction, crushing the small office across the aisle. Unfortunately for the chestnut horse, the loft floor had crashed into his stall. Only the jagged section of the side wall, which was supporting one end of the wooden floor at a sharp angle, had prevented the horse from being crushed and killed.

The three girls lined up along the high end of the floor section. "Lift and pull!" Stevie cried.

"Are you sure?" Lisa asked anxiously. "What if we hurt him?"

Carole grabbed the rough edge of the wood, hardly feeling the splinters that pierced her palms through her wool gloves. "We've got to try," she said. "If he keeps thrashing around under there he'll break his legs—or his back."

Lisa nodded and took hold. "Let's go," she said.

"One, two, three—pull!" Stevie cried.

The three girls threw all their strength into the task. The wooden boards creaked but held together. Then the boards started to slide slowly over the jagged wall. The chestnut horse let out another terrified squeal.

"It's coming!" Lisa shouted.

And it was. Within a couple of minutes, the girls had pulled the floor section completely clear of the stall. The far end slid off the stall's side wall, and the whole thing crashed harmlessly to the floor outside, raising another cloud of dust.

Stevie waved her hand in front of her face, coughing. "Is he okay?" she asked.

Carole had already gone to see. When she looked through the stall door, she groaned. The horse was still trapped! The loft floor section hadn't been the real culprit at all. It had merely been hiding the thick wooden support beam that was actually pinning the chestnut to the ground. When she looked more closely, Carole was pretty sure that the beam's weight wasn't actually resting on the horse. Like the floor section, it had gotten wedged on the way down—in this case, against the back corner of the stall. But it had obviously either knocked the horse off his feet or caught him resting in the straw. Either way, he was trapped now. The beam was only a fraction of an inch above his side, making it impossible for him to stand up or even roll over. The only thing he could do, now that the floor section was gone, was kick. And he was doing so enthusiastically, thrashing about with all four legs. Carole could tell that reaching the beam from the stall door wasn't going to be possible. Anyone who tried wouldn't get three steps before the horse kicked the life out of her—all four deadly hooves were aimed that way.

"Guys, we still have a problem," Carole called to her friends. In addition to his kicking, the horse was still neighing wildly, so she had to raise her voice to be heard.

Meanwhile, Lisa had just heard another voice over the racket the gelding was making. "Isn't that Elaine calling us?" she asked as she hurried to join Carole. She gasped when she saw their new problem. "Oh no!"

"One of us had better go see what Elaine wants," Stevie said. She was staring at the support beam.

"I'll go," Lisa offered.

As she started to clamber back over the rubble the way they had come, she noticed that there was a clearer path to the main entryway. One of the big double doors was hanging partway off its hinge. The opening was small, but so was Lisa. Within seconds, she was outside in the crisp winter air.

She raced around the side of the building, rounding the corner to find Elaine peering uncertainly into the back entry. This time the woman had both crutches. She still had Maxi with her in the carrier.

"Here I am," Lisa announced.

Elaine jumped and whirled around, almost unbalancing herself on her crutches. "Oh! I thought you were inside," she said.

"I was," Lisa said. "I came out the front. How's Maxi?"

Elaine glanced at the baby. "She's fine," she said. "She's been helping keep me calm, actually. But I tried to leave her alone just now, and she wasn't having any of it. She started bawling as soon as I headed for the door." The woman grimaced, then smiled. "I decided I'd better bring her with me, but I didn't want to take her into the building." She looked Lisa up and down, taking in her dirty, ripped coat and the layer of dust coating her face, hair, and hard hat. "How's it going?"

"Well, mostly great," Lisa said hesitantly.

"Mostly?" Elaine prompted. She glanced toward the paddock. The horses had calmed down. A few were drowsing or grazing, while others wandered about aimlessly, still restless from the excitement. "It looks like we're almost there."

"We've got all but one of them out," Lisa confirmed. Taking a deep breath, she explained the chestnut's situation.

Elaine gasped at the news. "Oh no!" she said. "I forgot! I did tell Jimmy to move Magoo into that box stall tonight."

"Magoo?" Lisa repeated.

Elaine nodded. "That's his name," she said, her voice worried. "You said he looks like he's still in one piece?"

"We think so," Lisa said. "The problem is getting him out. He's trapped pretty good, and he's really worked up, too."

Elaine absentmindedly straightened Maxi's hat, gazing at the barn worriedly. "I'm not surprised. He's not exactly our easiest customer even under ordinary circumstances. He's fussy and skittish and temperamental. Not vicious, you understand—he doesn't bite. But he's been known to kick when startled. And he's a big, strong horse. I don't know if you girls should risk getting too close."

"Don't worry," Lisa said. "We've handled skittish horses before. If there's a way to help Magoo, we'll find it."

Elaine shook her head slowly. "I'm not sure that's a good idea," she said, giving Lisa a serious look. "I think you'd better go tell your friends to leave him be. If the police arrive soon, maybe they can find a way to get him out."

Lisa couldn't believe what she was hearing. Leave a horse in danger and misery when they might be able to help him? Elaine had to be kidding! "And if they don't?" Lisa asked defiantly.

Elaine shrugged. "Well, I placed a call to Judy Barker when I was inside," she said. "She wasn't in, but I asked her to come whenever she got the message. If that's soon, she might be able to give Magoo an injection to calm him down so that we can dig him out."

Lisa nodded. That sounded like the most sensible plan to her. If the horse were tranquilized, freeing him would be no problem at all. They could just climb over him to get at the beam that had him trapped. "But it's New Year's Eve," Lisa said. "If Judy's out celebrating, she might not get the message for hours. What then?"

"I'm afraid I don't have any tranquilizers here at the moment." Elaine was speaking more slowly and reluctantly than ever. "But I do have something else I could use to put him down. I'd sooner put him out of his misery than let him freeze to death or kill himself by twisting a gut trying to get free."

Lisa gasped in horror. "No!" she exclaimed. The Saddle Club could still save Magoo. She had to make Elaine see that. Taking a deep breath, she got ready to argue.

Meanwhile, inside the building, Carole and Stevie were completely unaware that Magoo's life hung in the balance in more ways than one.

"Well, the good news is that his legs seem to be all right," Carole said wryly. The way the horse was kicking, it was obvious that all four limbs were in at least fair working order.

"Big help," Stevie said. Despite the freezing-cold air pouring in through the huge hole in the roof, she was warm from exertion. She unbuttoned Max's coat and stood back for a moment, surveying their options. "It's obvious we're not going in the front way."

Carole nodded. "Even if we could do it without getting kicked, I'm not sure we could reach the beam, anyway," she pointed out. While the beam came within a couple of feet of the ground in the back of the stall, the other end was resting on the far wall, which had remained intact and ended high above the girls' heads.

Stevie looked at the near wall, the one that had broken off in a jagged line about five feet up. "I wonder . . . ," she began.

At that moment Lisa reappeared, panting from running. "Bad news," she said, looking near tears.

Carole and Stevie listened with growing horror as Lisa explained Elaine's position.

"We can't just give up on him!" Carole cried.

Lisa bent over and put her hands on her knees, still fighting to regain her breath. "That's what I told her," she said. "But she wants us to come out right now and wait for Judy or the police."

Stevie was already shaking her head. "We can't do it," she said. "And she can't make us."

"That's true," Lisa said, perking up a little. "She won't bring the baby in here because she's afraid she'll get hurt. And she can't leave her inside—"

"Because Maxi won't let her!" Stevie exclaimed. She smiled for what felt like the first time in years. "See? Max the Fourth is already helping horses in need."

Carole wasn't smiling. She was looking worriedly over her shoulder at Magoo, who was still thrashing. "We'd better get moving," she said. "If we stay in here too long, Elaine might leave Maxi inside anyway and come in after us. It will take her a while on those crutches, but—"

"Enough said," Stevie said briskly. All three of them could already hear Elaine beginning to call to them again from outside. "Let's get to it."

Stevie turned to reexamine the problem. It still looked practically hopeless. There just wasn't enough room to squeeze by Magoo's flashing hooves. And even if there had been, the beam was too high. They would have to stand on each other's shoulders to reach it and push it aside.

That gave Stevie an idea. She turned again to examine the near wall. Even the remaining half was pretty high, and definitely solid. But maybe, just maybe . . .

"I've got it," Stevie cried suddenly, her eyes lighting up. "Superbaby!"

11

IT DIDN'T TAKE Stevie long to explain her plan. She had noticed a couple of things. First, she had observed that the beam was much lower on the near side and therefore would be fairly easy to move from that end, assuming that it wasn't too heavy to lift and that it wasn't jammed tight. Second, she had realized that as long as Magoo was trapped where he was, he couldn't roll over. That meant that the back corner of the stall, where the beam was lodged, was behind his back and thus safe from his hooves. Someone standing in that corner would be in no danger from the horse at all—as long as the beam was in place. The tricky parts were getting someone back there, then getting her out before the newly freed horse could roll over and kick her.

That had made Stevie remember her game with Maxi earlier that evening. She had made the baby "fly" by holding her legs. Couldn't The Saddle Club do the same sort of thing now? Two of their members could lower the third over the wall and hold her by the legs while she shifted the beam off the horse.

The others agreed that it was worth a try. And Lisa, as the lightest member of the group, had volunteered to play the part of Superbaby.

"Here goes nothing," she said as she pushed her way back into the hall next to Magoo's stall. She put her hands, still clad in their winter riding gloves, on top of the jagged wall, which was a few inches higher than her head. "Hoist me up."

Carole and Stevie each grabbed one of Lisa's ankles. On the count of three, they lifted with all their might.

Lisa helped out, gracefully pushing herself up with her hands. "Maybe those gymnastics classes my mom made me take did some good after all," she joked. Then she turned her attention to the task at hand.

She could feel her friends' hands gripping her legs tightly as she pushed herself farther over the wall. Soon her waist was bent over the top. But that wasn't going to be good enough.

"Give me some more height, guys," she called back.

Carole and Stevie obeyed, and soon Lisa was hanging awkwardly over the wall. An angled section along the top bit into her left leg, and the weight of her body resting against the wall was starting to cut off the circulation below her knees. But she hardly noticed. She was stretching down toward the beam.

Magoo obviously heard her. His ears twitched back and forth as he tried to figure out what was going on behind him. He let out a few more anxious neighs.

Lisa wasn't paying attention. She was concentrating on lengthening her body. Her joints protested as she balanced like a giant lever on top of the wall, reaching toward the beam. At least three feet of air still separated her fingertips from the closest section.

"Can you lower me any farther in?" she called back to her friends.

"I don't think so," Stevie shouted back. "We're having trouble hanging on as it is."

Lisa made one more reach, but she could already tell it was hopeless. "Pull me back," she said.

Soon she was resting on the messy floor of the neighboring stall. "I'm sorry," she gasped, rubbing her legs to restore circulation. "I just couldn't reach. But there's plenty of room back there in the corner. One of us could easily jump down there."

"Getting in isn't the problem," Carole pointed out. "It's getting out that's the hard part."

The others thought about that for a second. They all knew that in his present state, Magoo was likely to lash out at whomever he could reach. And once the beam was out of the way, that would be an immediate and deadly problem for anyone anywhere in the stall.

"Well," Lisa said at last, "we've got to try. I'll go in. Maybe if I can touch him, I can calm him down a little before I move the beam." She still couldn't bear to give up on the unfortunate horse. "And if not, maybe I can spring up to the top of the wall before he realizes he's free. Then you guys can drag me over."

"Are you sure you want to try this?" Carole asked uncertainly. It sounded awfully risky to her. Magoo didn't seem likely to calm down anytime soon. Still, she knew that Lisa was quite athletic. Maybe she *could* get out in time.

Lisa nodded firmly. There was a halter poking out of Carole's coat pocket, and Lisa grabbed it. "I'll take this in with me," she said. "Maybe I can get it on him. It might help me calm him down."

She tucked the halter in her own pocket and put her hands on the wall again. "Give me a boost," she said. "There's no time to lose."

The others knew how true that was. Once again, they hoisted Lisa up the broken wall. This time, they let go of her feet once she was up. She balanced again at the top for a second, like a gymnast on a bar. Then she swung her legs over the wall and dropped out of sight.

130

She landed lightly in the straw. Magoo heard and felt her landing and jerked his head in surprise. He let out a few more piercing cries.

"Don't worry, boy," Lisa said. "I'm here to help." She bent to examine the beam. It looked larger and more solid up close, but Lisa was pretty sure she could move it.

She scooted a little nearer to the horse. Soon she was close enough to reach out and touch his broad, sweaty back.

"It's okay, Magoo," she crooned. "Don't be so upset. You've got to stop kicking."

The horse jumped again at her first touch. But once again, his ears were pricked back in Lisa's direction, and he seemed to be listening to her.

Magoo's ears swiveled around to the front again when Carole's voice came from the stall doorway. "Is everybody okay in there?"

"Fine," Lisa called. "Magoo and I are just making friends. I'm going to try to get the halter on him now."

A few tense moments followed. Lisa had to lean forward over the horse's neck to get the halter on, putting her hands within reach of his big teeth. She prayed that Elaine was right in saying that the gelding didn't bite.

He didn't. He shook his head for a while, but eventually he held still long enough for Lisa to slip the halter on him and buckle it closed. She had already attached a lead line, which she drew back over his withers where she could reach the end when necessary. The horse actually seemed to calm down a bit when the halter was on. His legs slowed in their incessant pumping, and he snorted.

"I've got it," Lisa called to her friends. "I'm going to try to move the beam now."

She put both arms around the thick piece of wood and lifted. It was heavier than she had thought, but she managed to dislodge it from the corner and raise it an inch or two.

"He's thrashing harder again," Carole reported.

Stevie's head popped over the top of the broken-off wall. She had chinned herself up to see what was happening. "Can you lift it?" she asked.

Lisa couldn't spare the energy to look up. She gritted her teeth and did her best to hold on to the beam. If she dropped it now, it would most likely land squarely on Magoo's side. "Barely," she gasped.

Out of the corner of her eye, she could see that Carole was right. The horse was jerking around excitedly on the floor. If Lisa lifted the beam another few inches, he would be able to roll over, and that could be very bad news for both of them. Lisa could see now that the timing wasn't going to work. By the time she had moved the beam far enough to the side, the horse would certainly have rolled over and started kicking.

Lisa carefully lowered the beam, praying that it would

take hold again in the corner instead of falling on the horse. It did.

"I don't think this is going to work," she said. She felt tears welling up in her eyes. After all their efforts, would they have to give up? If only Magoo could understand that his fear was sealing his doom! If he were calmer, the girls could do it. The vet's tranquilizing shot would have done the trick. But the vet wasn't there.

Carole was peering into the stall. "He still looks pretty agitated," she said. "Maybe you should just get out of there."

Lisa gulped. "I feel like crying," she admitted to her friends, wiping the sweat off her forehead with the back of her hand. She did her best to crack a smile. "But I'm afraid if I do, my eyeballs will freeze solid."

"It *is* getting awfully cold in here," Carole said, staring at Magoo, who was covered with sweat.

Lisa could guess what her friend was thinking. If something didn't happen soon, Magoo would be in danger of dying from exposure.

Stevie had chinned herself up on the wall again. "Hey, it could be worse," she said. "It could be snowing." She jerked a thumb at the gaping hole in the roof above them. Unfortunately, the motion made her lose her balance, and she dropped out of sight again with a thump.

Lisa sighed. She knew that Stevie was just trying to

lighten the mood with a joke, but it wasn't working. "Who knows?" she said. "At this point I think I'd welcome a little snow. Maybe we could pack Magoo's legs in it so that he couldn't try to kill us while we're trying to save him."

"Good point," Carole said. "Let it snow!"

At that, despite the grimness of the situation, Stevie and Lisa couldn't resist. They both started humming the tune of "Let It Snow."

For a second, Lisa felt guilty about doing something as silly as humming during such a dire moment. But she figured a little music might calm her down and help her think of a new plan. She broke out singing on the first chorus, and Stevie joined in.

Carole looked a little surprised at first. Lisa could tell she didn't quite approve. But she and Stevie kept singing. And suddenly, Carole's expression changed.

"Don't look now, guys," she said, "but I think Magoo likes this song!"

Lisa looked down at the horse. His legs were still moving, but they were waving more slowly now. His ears were pricked in her direction.

Lisa's eyes widened. She thought Carole was right. She didn't dare say so, though, because she didn't dare stop singing. Stevie was back on top of the wall again, but she was singing, too. And on the next verse, Carole joined in.

When the girls ran out of words to the first song,

Stevie called out, "Okay, now let's do 'On Top of Old Smoky'!" The others followed her lead as she started to sing.

But Magoo didn't seem to approve. As soon as the girls started the new song, he tossed his head and started kicking harder again.

"Uh-oh," Carole said. "Maybe we should go back to 'Let It Snow.'"

Stevie stopped singing, too. "Maybe," she agreed. She paused, and a thoughtful look crossed her face. "Or maybe Magoo is just in the holiday spirit. Let's try another Christmas song."

Lisa rolled her eyes. "Come on, Stevie," she said. "We don't have time to experiment. Let's just stick with what we know works."

Stevie ignored her. She launched into "Jingle Bells," and the other two girls shrugged and joined in. Going along with Stevie's wild ideas was almost always easier than trying to resist them.

By the time they reached the second chorus, Magoo's legs were still. Only his ears were active, flicking around to try to listen to all three girls at once.

"I don't believe it," Carole said as she paused for breath before the chorus. "Stevie was right. Magoo *is* a real holiday horse!"

Stevie stopped singing as Carole started again. "I wonder if he only likes Christmas songs," she mused. "Maybe we should try 'Here Comes Peter Cottontail.'"

Both Carole and Lisa turned to give her a murderous glare. This time Stevie gave in meekly. She started singing "Jingle Bells" again at the top of her lungs.

Without speaking further, the girls knew what to do. Carole crept forward a short distance into the stall, still singing. Magoo watched her warily, but he kept still. Lisa leaned forward over his withers and tossed Carole the lead line. Carole caught it and scooted back out of harm's way, just as Stevie switched to "Rudolph the Red-Nosed Reindeer."

Lisa grasped the beam again. Her arms and shoulders were already aching, but she gathered her strength for one more round. Lifting slowly and carefully, she moved the beam up an inch, then two inches, then six inches. Meanwhile, Carole was tugging gently on the lead line. Now that Magoo was calmer, Lisa hoped that Carole could keep him from flipping over. She wished she could cross her fingers, but they were busy. And her toes were almost frozen in her boots. She concentrated harder.

It didn't take long for the horse to realize that he was finally free. He let out a few loud snorts, and his eyes started to roll as he wiggled against the floor. Carole started to sing even more loudly, and he flicked his ears toward her.

Lisa lifted the beam as high as she could to give the horse room to rise. As he scrambled to his feet, she dropped the beam beyond his hindquarters, then scurried for the side wall. Before Magoo had all four feet under him, Lisa was safe on the other side of the wall.

Carole kept a wary eye on the horse as he tossed his head. He seemed to be surprised to be on his feet again. He was still nervous, but the worst of his panic seemed to have passed. Still, by mutual though unspoken agreement, the girls kept singing until they had led him safely through the rubble, down the aisle, and out the door— right past an astonished-looking Elaine.

A FEW MINUTES later, the entire Hedgerow herd was on the move. Heeding Elaine's advice, Carole and Starlight were leading Magoo, who seemed too exhausted to cause much trouble. Most of the rest of the horses seemed happy enough to go along the wooded path. The girls had used the tail hitch method to tie one nervous two-year-old colt to the tail of the calm, steady Appaloosa mare that Carole had rescued.

Carole was at the front of the pack this time. Stevie, carrying Maxi, brought up the rear. Lisa kept Topside somewhere in the middle, urging along reluctant horses and soothing panicky ones.

And the whole way, the girls kept up a steady stream of festive holiday carols. Why mess with success?

Before they were halfway home, Lisa kept having to interrupt her singing to yawn. She couldn't remember the last time she had been so exhausted. And there was more work ahead. The horses would have to be groomed, checked and treated for injuries, and bedded down at Pine Hollow.

But that was okay. It would all be worth it. They had saved all the endangered horses—even Magoo.

As Carole launched into a rousing rendition of "Frosty the Snowman," Lisa yawned again and glanced at her watch. She was surprised to see that it was after one o'clock in the morning.

"Hey, you guys," she called out, interrupting her own singing. "Happy New Year!"

Carole and Stevie paused, too. "Wow," Carole called back. "I guess we missed midnight."

Stevie didn't say anything. Lisa held Topside back for a minute, allowing Belle to catch up to them. "Did you hear what I said?" Lisa asked, glancing over her shoulder as a couple of Hedgerow stragglers passed by. The horses looked almost as tired as Lisa felt, and she smothered another yawn.

"Shhh," Stevie said, putting a finger to her lips. She pointed to her front.

Lisa looked and saw Maxi nestled in the carrier. Her eyes were closed and her small shoulders under their layers of clothing rose and fell rhythmically.

"Well, what do you know?" Lisa whispered. "Maxi the Super-awake-baby finally fell asleep!"

Stevie grinned. "It must have been our singing," she

whispered back. "It's been known to work miracles, you know."

Before Lisa could answer, Stevie launched into "Joy to the World."

Lisa shrugged and joined in. A second later, Carole did, too. All three of the girls knew that they had good reason to be joyful.

As the odd herd emerged from the tree line behind Max's house, The Saddle Club found helpers waiting for them.

"There they are!" someone shouted.

Carole squinted. Her eyes felt raw, and her head was throbbing. All she could think about was falling into bed and sleeping for a week. It took her a second to recognize Judy Barker. Max and Deborah were right behind the vet.

Max and Judy hurried forward, each of them taking hold of a couple of halters and leading the Hedgerow horses down the hill. The stable was lit up as bright as day, as was the house. Meanwhile, Deborah was coming toward the girls with an anxious look on her face. She soon spotted Maxi slumbering in the infant carrier.

"Maxi!" she cried, running toward Belle. Stevie was already unhooking the carrier and preparing to hand the baby to her mother.

Deborah hugged Maxi tight, then hooked the carrier around her own shoulders. The baby opened her eyes and blinked sleepily for a few seconds. Then her eyes fell closed again and she let out a little snore and murmur.

Stevie was starting to feel more than a little anxious about their escapade. Would Deborah be angry that they had taken her baby along on this cold cross-country ride? Stevie knew they had really had no choice, but she wasn't sure Deborah would agree. Deborah certainly had a very odd expression on her face at the moment.

"Stevie!" Max shouted from somewhere down the hill. "Don't just sit there. Get down here and start making up some stalls for these horses."

Stevie slid down off Belle. In her free hand she grabbed the halter of the Appaloosa mare, which had stopped nearby to graze on the winter-frozen lawn. Belle, the Appaloosa, and the tail-hitched colt all followed obediently as she hurried toward the stable. She would just have to deal with Deborah later.

SOME TIME LATER, Max, Judy, and The Saddle Club staggered up the hill and into the house. The girls were so tired by then that they could hardly stay on their feet. But every one of the Hedgerow horses was safe, sound, and snug inside the stable.

Inside the house, they found Deborah waiting with a tray of steaming hot cocoa and a plate of cookies.

"They're left over from Christmas," she said apologetically. "They may be a little stale."

The weary workers didn't mind. They quickly gobbled down every one. Max paused just long enough to call Elaine and assure her that everything was okay.

"So," Max said after the first frenzy of eating had passed, "I guess it's a good thing Deborah and I were too tired to stay in town for the second half of the show."

Judy nodded. "And I'm glad my husband and I were just at a party here in Willow Creek," she said. "I was home by a little after twelve-thirty. When I called Elaine, she said you girls had just left, so I came straight over here."

"Are all the horses going to be okay?" Carole asked the vet anxiously.

Judy nodded. "I think so," she said. "A couple of them have some minor injuries, and that chestnut is cut up pretty badly. I'll have to check on them in the morning. But I think they'll all come out of it okay."

"Thanks to you three," Max added, smiling at The Saddle Club. "I'm proud of what you did out there tonight."

"Thanks, Max," the girls said in one voice.

"Although I do have one bone to pick with you," Max added.

"What's that?" Stevie asked. She wondered if Max was annoyed that they had taken Topside. He was one of Pine Hollow's most valuable horses.

Max grinned. "It's just that I hoped I'd be there to see my daughter take her very first ride."

Everyone laughed. Stevie noticed that even Deborah was smiling. "Does this mean you're not mad at us?" Stevie asked her.

Deborah shrugged. "What can I say?" she said. "I never thought my seven-month-old would be going on a midnight trail ride on New Year's Eve."

Stevie wasn't sure that Deborah had answered her question. But she decided to let it be. If Deborah was angry, Stevie for one was too tired to deal with it right then.

She settled back against the couch cushions with a groan. Now that she had thawed out from the winter cold, every bone and muscle in her body was starting to ache. "Remind me never to do that again," she said. "I wouldn't even have gotten this beat up at Chad's party. Probably."

Judy chuckled and checked her watch. "I'd better get going," she said. "I'll drop you girls off at your homes if you like."

"Thanks, Judy," Carole said gratefully. "We were supposed to spend the night here, but somehow sleeping on

143

the living room floor doesn't sound as appealing as it did earlier today."

Max laughed. "Don't worry, you can consider your baby-sitting duties officially done. We'll take over from here."

The Saddle Club and Judy stood and started to gather their things.

"Can we say good night to Maxi before we go?" Lisa asked Deborah tentatively. "If you don't think we'll disturb her, that is." After what they had been through trying to tire out the baby, the last thing Lisa wanted to do was wake her up.

Deborah headed toward the stairs, gesturing for the girls to follow. "Come on," she said. "I don't think you have to worry about waking her."

The girls soon saw what she meant. When they tiptoed into the nursery, the night-light illuminated the crib just enough for them to get a good look at Maxi. The baby was on her back, her head tipped slightly to one side. Her arms were splayed out on either side of her body. Her eyes were closed tight, her mouth was open slightly, and her chest moved up and down in slow, rhythmic motions.

Carole smiled. "She must be exhausted," she whispered.

Deborah leaned on the side of the crib and gazed down at her daughter fondly. "She had a lot of excitement tonight," she replied quietly.

"I hope you're not annoyed with us about that," Carole

said, giving Deborah an anxious glance. "Lisa was going to stay here with her, but we didn't think we could—"

"It's okay," Deborah said, cutting Carole off. She reached down to brush a stray hair off Maxi's cheek, then turned to smile at the girls. "I read your note, and I know you didn't have a choice. You had to help Elaine, and you did. Even though it meant turning Maxi into an early rider."

"So you're not mad at us?" Carole asked.

"I'm not mad at you. And I'm not mad that Maxi has already been on horseback." She laughed. There was a twinkle in her eye that made The Saddle Club realize that their holiday gift had worked. Deborah had relaxed—and regained her sense of humor. "After all," she said, "it was only a matter of time."

"DID YOU NOTICE that mare?" Stevie asked, pointing to the calm Appaloosa from Hedgerow. It was a week later. The Saddle Club was leaning on the rails of the outdoor ring with Britt Lynn, watching as several Hedgerow stable hands loaded their horses onto a large van. The cold snap had broken, and the new Hedgerow stable was almost finished. After the collapse of the roof, Elaine had hired extra builders to rush the job as much as possible.

Britt nodded and watched as the Appaloosa strode up the ramp without hesitation. "She's pretty," the girl offered shyly.

"Elaine told me her name is Applesauce," Carole said.

She pointed to another Hedgerow horse, a stocky bay. "And that's Jasper."

This time Britt just nodded. Carole sighed. The Saddle Club had been spending as much time as possible with the new girl over the past few days. They wanted to get to know her quickly so that they would be able to do a better job of finding her the right horse. But Britt was still so shy that it wasn't going too well so far.

Stevie had decided to take another tack. "So, tell us a little about your old horse, Britt," she said. "Toledo, isn't it? What was he like?"

"Um, he was great," Britt said. "I'll tell you about him some other time, okay? I've got to go."

She slipped away before the other girls could protest. Lisa watched her go, feeling frustrated.

"She's not making this easy, is she?" she commented.

Carole had turned away to watch as Elaine emerged from the stable. As soon as the woman spotted The Saddle Club, she swung toward them on her crutches.

"There you are," she said when she reached them. "I was looking for you. I wanted to thank you girls again in person for all you've done. I don't know how to thank you enough."

"We're glad to have been able to help," Lisa replied politely. Her friends nodded.

Elaine smiled. "Well, you certainly did help," she said. "I owe you one. I know you're terribly loyal to old Max there"—she gestured toward Max, who had just led the

146

last of the horses out of the stable—"but if you ever want a change of pace, you're always welcome to try out any of my horses you want. No charge."

"Thanks," Carole said. "We might just take you up on that sometime. You've got some great horses."

"Yes, I do," Elaine said, a look of wonder crossing her face. "Even after all that's happened this year, I guess I do."

"You have had some bad luck, haven't you?" Stevie said before she could stop herself. Realizing that her comment hadn't been very tactful, she tried to correct it. "Um, I mean, well, that is, I meant, uh, you know . . ."

Elaine laughed so hard that one of her crutches slipped. "I know," she said. "But they say these things happen in threes, right? And I've had three in a row: first the swamp fever, then my leg, then the roof. So I figure I'm about due for some *good* luck for a change."

The Saddle Club had to agree with that.

They walked Elaine back toward the van, moving slowly because of her crutches. "I think maybe your good luck has already started," Carole pointed out. "All your horses came through this safe and sound."

"True," Elaine said. "Judy gave most of them a clean bill of health this morning. And she's pretty sure Magoo will be fine in the end, too. She wants him to stay put for another week or two to avoid aggravating his wounds. But she said it's really just a precaution."

Judy Barker had recommended that Magoo remain at

Pine Hollow until his condition improved. During his ordeal, the chestnut horse had gotten quite a few bruises and cuts on his legs and body, and the skin on his side had been rubbed raw where it had been pressed against the floor. None of the injuries was terribly serious in itself, but because there were so many of them, Judy wanted to play it safe.

"Well, we already told you," Stevie said. "We're going to be on call as Magoo's volunteer nurses as long as he's here."

Elaine chuckled. "You might change your minds about that," she said with a bemused expression on her face. "I'm crazy about old Magoo. But I must admit, he isn't the easiest guy in the world to get along with."

"Don't worry," Carole said. "Before long we'll be his best friends."

Elaine laughed again. Then, as the van driver called to her, she thanked the girls again and left. The van chugged into gear, and the girls waved as it started to pull off down Pine Hollow's gravel driveway.

Elaine rolled down the passenger-side window and leaned out. "Just give me a ring if you have any trouble with him," she called.

"Okay!" Stevie called back. The girls watched until the van had turned onto the road at the foot of the driveway; then they went inside.

"Time for our visit to the patient," Carole announced

cheerfully. "We can't let him get lonely here at beautiful Pine Hollow Horse Hospital."

"Speaking of lonely," Lisa said as the girls turned down the stable row toward the stall that was Magoo's temporary home, "I can't help thinking that Britt must be awfully lonely. She just moved, and she's so shy . . ."

"I know what you mean," Carole said. "We really should try to draw her out of her shell. It's not easy moving to a new state in the middle of the school year."

Stevie nodded. "Let's make it a Saddle Club project," she suggested. "For starters, we could ask her to be on our team for the gymkhana."

"Good idea," Lisa said. The gymkhana was only a little over a week away now. "We'll do our best to be extra nice to her in the meantime."

Carole nodded. "Make her feel really welcome here at Pine Hollow—maybe help her make some friends. It will be fun."

Stevie grinned over her shoulder at her friends as she swung open Magoo's stall door. "And *not* just because we might get to help pick out her new horse!"

They all knew that Brittney would be the next Saddle Club project.

ABOUT THE AUTHOR

Bonnie Bryant is the author of nearly a hundred books about horses, including The Saddle Club series, Saddle Club Super Editions, and the Pony Tails series. She has also written novels and movie novelizations under her married name, B. B. Hiller.

Ms. Bryant began writing The Saddle Club in 1986. Although she had done some riding before that, she intensified her studies then and found herself learning right along with her characters Stevie, Carole, and Lisa. She claims that they are all much better riders than she is.

Ms. Bryant was born and raised in New York City. She still lives there, in Greenwich Village, with her two sons.

Don't miss Bonnie Bryant's next exciting
Saddle Club Adventure . . .

HORSE GUEST
The Saddle Club #73

The Saddle Club has two projects! They are helping
Brittney Lynn find the perfect horse and taking care
of a not-so-perfect horse, Magoo. Unfortunately,
Magoo's a very demanding patient. He wants all The
Saddle Club's attention, and he wants it now. How
can they help Britt when Magoo is taking all their
time? As their frustration mounts, The Saddle Club
begins to wish this four-legged guest would go back
where he belongs!

Meanwhile, Stevie's grandmother is visiting the
Lakes, and the kids have promised to be on their best
behavior. Can Stevie and her brothers keep their
resolution? Will the Lakes' unusual behavior send
their two-legged guest running for home?